Presented to

Moonie

with love,

From

Eric & Melissa

By Helen Steiner Rice

Helen Steiner Rice

Remembering With Love

Collector's Edition

Fleming H. Revell Company
Old Tappan, New Jersey

Compiled and edited by Norma F. Chimento
Researched by Virginia J. Ruehlmann
Illustrated by Cassandre Maxwell
Frontispiece by Eileen Annest

Library of Congress Cataloging in Publication Data

Rice, Helen Steiner.
    Remembering with love Helen Steiner Rice.

    I. Title.
PS3568.I28A6   1985   813'.54   84-27703
ISBN 0-8007-1434-2

Contents

Publisher's Foreword

To chronicle the life and outreach of Helen Steiner Rice in one book is about as hard as capturing a sunbeam in a jar. Radiant, sometimes elusive, yet always warm and beaming bright, the influence this woman continues to have around the world is phenomenal.

How many people shivering with loneliness have been warmed by her words? How many birthdays, anniversaries, holidays have been brightened by the sentiments she wrote? Remembered? And cherished? How many tears have been dried, conflicts resolved, reconciliations wrought, and hopes restored? The personal files and papers which we explore are silent confirmation.

Her faith was simple—"childlike" she called it—and unwavering. It permeated everything she did. Her life remains an emblem of the love she expressed in word and deed for all people in all walks of life.

In this latest book, *Remembering With Love,* we have tried to do just that—remember Helen, with love. We went to six of her close friends and associates and asked them to share a special remembrance. They graciously consented; each capturing a different facet of her life and offering a new, sometimes unheralded insight into her character. Her sister, Gertrude, begins by recalling their childhood.

Each chapter opens with a brief introduction to the theme. It is followed by a personal remembrance. Next is some of Helen's most inspiring prose, taken from her extensive correspondence, her books, and newspaper and magazine articles, on the same subject. Finally, we added the poems, including some of her early attempts, the most notable of which is a lovely one dedicated to her mother, "Life's Fairest Flower." (These are identified as HES for Helen Elaine Steiner.) There are later works as well, including some rife with humor.

We hope that this book would have been well received by Helen herself. She was a perfectionist and vitally involved in all of her publications.

In researching and compiling the material at hand, we came upon a poem that—to the best of our knowledge—has never before appeared in print. It seemed to allay our misgivings and communicate her foregone acceptance of our *Remembering With Love.*

MEMORY RENDEZVOUS

Memory builds a little pathway
That goes winding through my heart.
It's a lovely, quiet, gentle trail
From other things apart;
I only meet when traveling there
The folks I like the best
For this Road I call REMEMBRANCE
Is hidden from the rest;
But I hope I'll always find you
In my MEMORY RENDEZVOUS
For I keep this little secret place
To meet with folks like YOU.

Our special thanks to Virginia J. Ruehlmann for her sensitive and unending efforts in researching and providing the material from Helen's papers. Our gratitude also to Eileen Annest for permitting us to reproduce her beautiful pastel portrait of Helen, a gift on the celebration of her eightieth birthday, May 19, 1980.

Norma F. Chimento
Managing Editor

Introduction

It was my privilege to be assigned responsibility for reviewing the voluminous files, records, and writings of Helen Steiner Rice for the purpose of cataloging. What started out as a monumental task turned into a delightful and rewarding experience, for through Helen's writings she revealed much of her character and many personality traits.

During Helen's lifetime, her goal was to live each day according to Christ's principles and to "never consciously hurt anybody in any way." Her ambition was "to do as much good as I can, as often as I can, in as many places as I can." She was a giving, caring, loving, sharing individual.

High ideals, integrity, and spiritual values were important to her. She was a woman of strong conviction. When she believed in a cause or an individual, or sensed an injustice had been committed, she was tenacious in standing up for her position, her friend, or her belief, and persevering in righting the wrong.

Helen Steiner Rice was blessed with a simple, childlike faith that permitted her to reach out to others and to be understood. Her supreme faith in God, her zestful attitude toward life, and her unshakable love of all mankind were constantly demonstrated through her many acts of concern, generosity, kindness, and thoughtfulness. She, who had known heartbreak and suffering, sustained others through their personal crises and "heart-hurts." She offered comfort and encouragement, and gave abundantly of her time, talent, and self to so many in need.

She was peppy and witty. She was spunky and courageous. She was considerate and sincere.

Her writings—prose and poetry, some previously published, some unpublished—possess the ability to mesmerize the reader. Her works instill an inner calm, a welcome serenity. The pen of Helen Steiner Rice generates comfort, faith, and peace.

Some years ago she wrote:

"You can't pluck a rose all fragrant with dew,
Without some of the fragrance remaining on you."

Permit me to paraphrase that:

You can't read a poem by Helen Steiner Rice
Without some of the inspiration and love touching you.

Enjoy the aroma—the fragrance remains forever!

Virginia J. Ruehlmann

1

Helen and Her Family

Helen Elaine Steiner was the first of two daughters born to John and Anna Bieri Steiner at the turn of the century.

By virtue of its number, theirs was a small, closely knit family unit. Helen often described her and her sister Gertrude's early childhood as "happy and secure," and her personalized account of their kith and kin is carried in this first chapter.

But Helen had an extended family as well. It consisted of her many friends, her co-workers, her readers, their children and associates, and, in time, their successors. She needed little prompting to respond to requests for rhyming remembrances of the important events in their lives.

And she never defaulted.

The poetry selections included here reflect the waves of affection that flowed from her very own, immediate family and became a wellspring of love for her extended family.

Anna

Helen

Gertrude

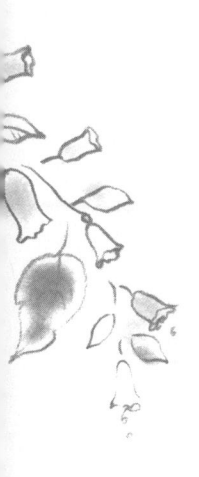

Remembering Helen

If my sister, Helen, had one outstanding character trait, it had to be her friendly nature expressed by her concern for others. As young girls, one of our pastimes was to take long walks through our neighborhood in Lorain, Ohio, and into the downtown area. These excursions provided her with the right occasion to spread a little cheer among all those people we encountered — young and old. Helen was particularly fond of the older folks, and she was extremely nice to them, inquiring about their health, their children, and other concerns.

She was my "big" sister, in terms of age, not of size (we were both about the same height — five foot one), but she never pulled her rank. She was always thoughtful, considerate, loving.

Helen had a pet name for me. Frankly, I don't know how she came by it. It was Pedro, and she used it frequently.

At the time of the death of her husband, Franklin, certainly a heartbreaking experience for her, she accepted the challenge to move forward and not wallow in self-pity. Her deep faith helped her through that terrible ordeal. Perhaps knowing that her mother and her sister were at her side was a consolation, too.

If I were to choose one word to describe Helen, it is perfect.

Gertrude M. Steiner

Dear Friends,

When admirers of my verse write to ask me personal questions about my family background, I am not very expansive, and with good cause. I simply don't know much about my roots. It's not very important in God's eyes — man's financial worth, his knowledge or his parentage — so why should it be in ours? The primary question we need to answer is, "How are we using the life God gave us?" If we are engaged in living for His glory and the good of others around us, then our lives speak well of us and do honor to our forebears. Having made that point, let me say that I was blessed with hardy, healthy, honest, hardworking ancestors.

My mother, Anna Bieri, was born of first-generation parents who immigrated here in the late 1800s from Bern, Switzerland. They settled on a small farm near Wooster, Ohio. The land there was not the best, so the Bieris had to struggle to make a living, something that soured my mother on farm life forever. When her sister married an artist and moved to Cleveland, she vowed to follow, and she did as soon as she had finished high school.

My father, John A. Steiner, was born of German stock, his parents owning a very successful dairy farm near Sterling, Ohio, not far from Wooster. The Steiners' cattle were some of the finest around, and I am told that their well-painted house and barns drew approving comments from all who rode past in their horse-drawn buggies.

Of all my grandparents, only Grandma Bieri has a special place in my memory. That is because she lived with our family in Lorain from time to time. After her husband died, she moved from child to child, staying with one for a while, then another.

What a dear woman she was, a real old-fashioned grandma. Stooped and wearied from all her years of hard work on the farm, she still had a wonderful spirit and deep Christian faith. She also had a big lap on which I sat at every opportunity. When she was staying with us, I'd make a beeline for her room after school and excitedly tell her of the day's happenings. She listened with the full attention only grandmas have time to give. Always, I'd find her bent over her large German Bible, which rested on a stand near the window. She studied God's Word by the hour. Not good with the English language, even after a lifetime in America, Grandma Bieri got by with a few words of approval, a wonderfully accepting smile, and a love that was irrepressible.

On Sunday nights, we'd have our family worship time. That was one of the blessings of a radioless, televisionless era: there was time for family conversation. Without fail, I'd climb up on a chair and preach, using all the Bible verses I knew. This pleased my grandma greatly, and with adoring eyes she would tell Mother in German, "How that girl can preach!"

One of the saddest times in my early childhood came when Grandma fell and hurt herself. My sister, Gertrude, and I were out walking with her in the nearby woods. When we tried to cross a stream that ran through them, Grandma Bieri slipped and broke her arm.

I cried a prayer that night that God would heal her quickly—which in time He did. Grandma tried only to minimize her discomfort, embarrassed that she'd caused so much commotion. She was always afraid that she would impose on our family and be a nuisance. Her selflessness was an inspiration to all and a testimony to the faith she held so close. Without fail, she was always concerned about others.

HSR

Excerpt from In the Vineyard of the Lord
by Helen Steiner Rice,
copyright ©1979 by Helen Steiner Rice and Fred Bauer.
Published by Fleming H. Revell Company.

LIFE'S FAIREST FLOWER

I have a garden within my soul,
     Of wondrous beauty rare,
Wherein the blossoms of all my life,
     Bloom ever in splendor fair.

The fragrance and charm of that garden,
     Where all of life's flowers bloom,
Fills my aching heart with sweet content,
     And banishes failure's gloom.

Each flower a message is bringing,
     A mem'ry of someone dear,
A picture of deepest devotion,
     Dispelling all doubt and fear.

Amid all this beauty and splendor,
     One flower stands forth as queen—
Alone in her dazzling beauty,
     Alone but ever supreme.

This flower of love and devotion,
     Has guided me all thru life,
Softening my grief and my sorrow,
     Sharing my toil and my strife.

This flower has helped me to conquer,
     Temptation so black and grim,
And led me to victory and honor,
     Over my enemy—SIN.

I have vainly sought in my garden,
     Thru blossoms of love and light,
For a flower of equal wonder,
     To compare with this one so bright.

But ever I've met with failure,
     My search has been in vain—
For never a flower existed,
     Like the blossom I can claim.

For after years I now can see,
        Amid life's roses and rue,
God's greatest gift—to a little child,
        My darling MOTHER was YOU.
                        HES

HAPPY ANNIVERSARY

Whenever I write about weddings
        and a happy married life,
I always use as a PATTERN
        my "favorite husband and wife."
I start with a day in OCTOBER
        by recalling a beautiful bride
And a happy, handsome bridegroom,
        standing proudly at her side.
Then through the years I follow
        the life of this wonderful pair.
And watch them sharing together
        their moments of PLEASURE and PRAYER.
Then I think of their BEAUTIFUL CHILDREN
        and their CHILDREN'S CHILDREN, too,
For they are living examples
        of what TOGETHERNESS can do.
They're symbols of everything DECENT
        and everything FINE and GOOD,
A family that lives for each other
        the way that all families should,
And THIRTY-FOUR YEARS have just proven
        what nobody can disparage,
It takes a lot of FAITH and LOVE
        to make a HAPPY MARRIAGE,
And it takes a lot of praying
        and a devoted husband and wife
To keep GOD EVER PRESENT
        in their HAPPY FAMILY LIFE!

AT MY MOTHER'S KNEE

I have worshipped in CHURCHES and CHAPELS
I have PRAYED in the BUSY STREET
I have sought MY GOD and have found HIM
Where the waves of the ocean beat....
I have knelt in a silent forest
In the shade of an ancient TREE.....
But the dearest of all my altars
Was raised at MY MOTHER'S KNEE.
God make me the woman of HER VISION
And purge me of all SELFISHNESS
And KEEP ME TRUE TO HER STANDARDS
And HELP me to LIVE to BLESS
And then keep me a PILGRIM FOREVER....
To the shrine at my Mother's Knee.

MY OWN DEAR DAD

He's always quick to understand,
He always lends a helping hand,
He shares my problems and my play,
And helps me many times a day,
He believes in me, when others doubt,
He's a loyal pal and a grand, good scout,
All that I am or hope to be,
All that is "GOOD" that happens to me,
I Owe to my DAD...
        and MOM would agree,
For Dad Picked Her Out and Gave Her to Me.
So HERE's to MY DAD, and may I be....
        As Kind to Him as He's Been to Me.

WHERE DOES THE TIME GO?

WHERE does TIME go in its endless flight?
Spring turns to Fall and Day to Night!
And little girls grow up and marry
For years fly by and do not tarry:
And though it seems but yesterday
That P — was busily at play
The months and years have quickly flown
And your "small doll" is now "full grown"
And instead of pinafores and curls
She's joined the ranks of "married girls."

I simply can't believe it's true
And I know it's hard for you folks, too
To realize YOUR BABY'S grown
And that the "little bird" has flown
And left behind "an empty place"
The "rosebud's" gone...there's just the "vase"
And rooms that rang with laughing song
Are "softly quiet" all day long.

The years go by on jet-lined wings
And take away our "treasured things"
And leave us only "empty hands"
And feet that stand on "sinking sands"
But life's an ever-changing force
We cannot alter Nature's course....
For Tides cannot be kept from flowing
Or restless winds be stilled when blowing
And no one can hold back the dawn
Or wipe the dewdrops from the lawn
For life's an always-changing thing
And each new day is sure to bring
New problems we must learn to face
With quiet dignity and grace!

FOR GERTRUDE, A WONDERFUL SIS

If I knew the place
      WHERE WISHES COME TRUE,
That's where I would go
      for My Wish For You,
And I'd wish you all
      that YOU'RE WISHING FOR,
For no sister on earth
      deserves it more,
But trials and troubles
      come to us all,
For that's the way
      we grow "Heaven Tall,"
And My Birthday Prayer
      to Our Father Above
Is to Keep You Safe
      In His Infinite Love,
And we both know
      that GIFTS DON'T MEAN MUCH
Compared to "Our Love"
      and God's Blessed Touch!

TO MY FAVORITE NURSE'S MOTHER

You "Mother" every living thing
From poodle dogs to birds that sing.
You give a Mother's tender care
To marigolds and maiden-hair.
You gently nurture tiny seeds
And help fulfill their growing needs.
You pet and pamper "pale tomatoes"
And fondle onions and potatoes.
All growing things get your attention
And much, much more than I can mention.
You lend your many loving ways
And spread your sunny little rays
Among God's creatures everywhere
And give them all a Mother's care....
So on this day that honors MOTHERS
I honor ONE WHO CARES FOR OTHERS—
I'm sending MY LOVE along with this verse
to the mother of "My Favorite Nurse."

TO THE NEW MOTHER AND FATHER
FROM THE PROUD AND HAPPY GRANDPARENTS

We're happy for you both, because
Your precious baby's birth
Is sure to make your happy home
A bit of heaven on earth...
For there's nothing like a baby
So cuddly, small, and sweet,
To give life added meaning
And make it more complete...
And, of course, we're mighty selfish
In OUR happiness for YOU,
Because, you see, dear children,
You've made us happy, too...
For there's nothing like a Grandchild
To boast of and adore
And to bring back precious memories
Of your babyhood, once more...
And with our loving wishes
Comes a deep and heartfelt prayer:
"God keep YOU and YOUR BABY
Safely in HIS DAILY CARE."

A WEE BIT OF HEAVEN

A wee bit of heaven
Drifted down from above,
A handful of happiness,
A heart full of love;

The MYSTERY of LIFE
So sacred and sweet,
The GIVER of JOY
So deep and complete;

Precious and priceless,
So lovable, too,
The world's sweetest MIRACLE
BABY————is you.

WELCOME, DEAR BABY

Welcome, Dear Baby, to a world that is NEW
...you've been eagerly awaited by your MOM and
DAD, too!

You're starting life surrounded by LOVE ON
EVERY SIDE...and your MOM and DAD behold you
with PLEASURE and with PRIDE...you've embarked
on a VENTURE that is VERY STRANGE and NEW
...and you have to get acquainted with the
world surrounding you...but with such great
parents to introduce you, dear...you'll soon get
used to living VERY HAPPILY down here!

You will have a lot of SUNNY DAYS and many
BRIGHT and HAPPY HOURS...but remember, dear,
with SUNSHINE there will always be some
SHOWERS...for life must be a mixture both of
SUNSHINE and of RAIN...of JOY and of SORROW
mixed with PLEASURE and with PAIN...but GOD
WILL ALWAYS BE THERE to HELP and BLESS YOU,
too...as you grow into MANHOOD and ALL YOUR
DREAMS COME TRUE!

And in everything you do, remember to
be KIND...and may you look at people with
YOUR HEART, not just your mind...for remember
OUR CREATOR LOOKS DOWN FROM HEAVEN ABOVE...
so LIVE ALWAYS in "HIS LIKENESS" and LEARN TO
SHARE HIS LOVE!

So, WELCOME, DEAR BABY, to this world STRANGE
and NEW...and GOD BLESS YOUR FAMILY, who
are all "IN LOVE WITH YOU"!

HAPPY BIRTHDAY TO RICHARD'S MOTHER!

I don't know you, that is true...and yet I
almost feel I do. For MOTHERS' HEARTS are
all the same...regardless of their family
name. And I can't help but feel inside,
how your heart beamed with love and pride,
when Richard showed his notes to you and
shared his honors with you too. And now that
you are EIGHTY-ONE. I think the praise your
son has won is just a BRIGHT REFLECTION,
dear, of the WONDERFUL MOTHER who brought him
here. For children build their lives the way,
their mothers teach them, day by day. And
ALL THEY ARE and ALL THEY DO, they owe to
MOTHERS just like YOU. And so today we
honor YOU, for YOUR FAITH helped your boy to
do—The "RIGHT THINGS"—for you made him
strong and taught him what was RIGHT and
WRONG. Without a Mother's LOVE and
DEVOTION, no man would ever win promotion.
You taught him the fundamentals of life, and
placed him then in the hands of his wife.
And together, whatever your son has won, you
both can consider that you have done. So let
me bow and salute you, dear, as you enter into
your EIGHTY-FIRST YEAR...To you all credit
and honor is due, for your children's honors
belong to you. For you live in your children
and what they do, because they are just a
PART of YOU. And here is a wish that our
dear God above, will bless you today with the
GIFT of HIS LOVE!

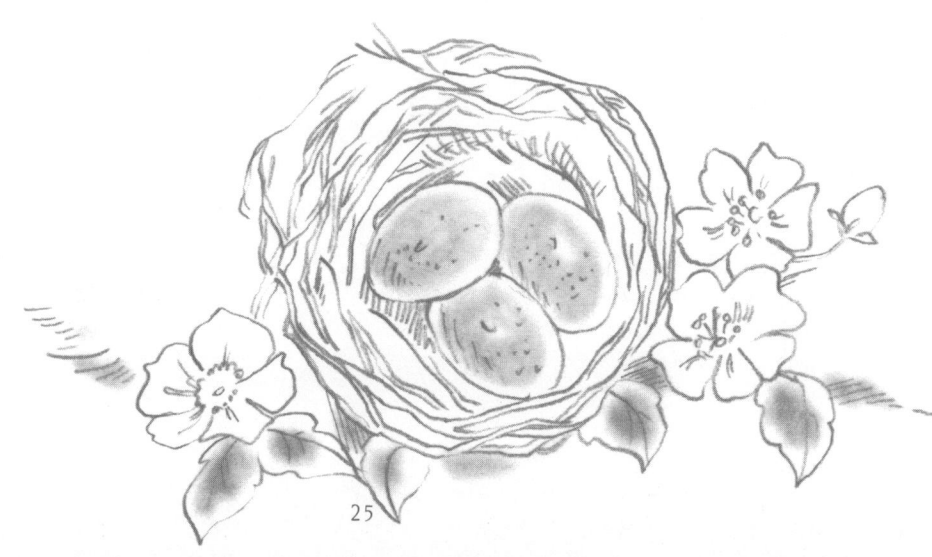

2

Helen, the Friend and Giver of Gifts

Conjecture has it that no better knowledge of a woman can be had than by living with her. We would add a qualifing phrase—or by working with her.

Mary Jo Eling served as secretary to Helen for over twelve years. Her services were regarded as superior and her dedication unwavering.

One day, in the usual mound of incoming correspondence, Helen found a letter from a Sister Mary Felicitas who inquired if there were something she could do to repay the poet for her poems and the joy and comfort they afforded the nun.

She showed the letter to Mary Jo who recognized the writer as one of her high-school teachers.

"Well," replied Helen, "in that case Sister Mary has already repaid me by sending you to help." And she so reaffirmed in a letter of reply.

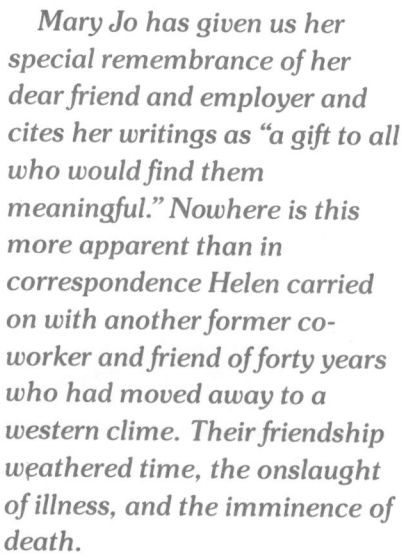

Mary Jo has given us her special remembrance of her dear friend and employer and cites her writings as "a gift to all who would find them meaningful." Nowhere is this more apparent than in correspondence Helen carried on with another former co-worker and friend of forty years who had moved away to a western clime. Their friendship weathered time, the onslaught of illness, and the imminence of death.

In the excerpts that we have selected, you will discover the great rapport that existed between the two and will recognize the courage that mutually sustained them.

Remembering Helen

"To know me, " Mrs. Rice would often say, "just read my writings." Her values, her beliefs, and all that was important to her made their way into prose and poetry. She could put into expression all that she wanted to share with others. And she had much to share...a deep faith, eternal hope, and universal love. This was her whole life...to reach out to others with this God-given talent. She wrote sincerely and genuinely, disclosing her very self. And because she did, her writings have become a gift to all who find them meaningful.

Mary Jo Eling

Editor's Note: One of the things I have always held sacred is a person's privacy: it is a practice in our home never to open the mail of another family member.

And so, when I was to research the files and papers of Helen Steiner Rice, I had to overcome my natural reticence and habit of long standing. Some of what I found in that initial investigation in August 1983—and the related material Virginia J. Ruehlmann later supplied—constitute the "Chasey" letters that follow. A portion of them are offered in short excerpts, and others are run in their completeness: they cover a period of twenty-eight months. Only Helen's letters are included.

I now feel that reprinting them is not an intrusion of the friends' privacy, but rather a glorious opportunity to gain an insight into their lives and thinking, and vicariously to climb the same peaks and walk in the same valleys, to share the hope and feel the despair, to become a partner in the prayer and intercession.

September 14, 1972

DEAR, DEAR, DEAR "CHASEY,"

Here I am engulfed in perhaps one of the "darkest hours" of my life. We have often discussed these "dark hours of SOUL SEARCHING," and they come as nothing strange or unexpected, for we know this is the way of life. But somehow, as we grow older, they do increase in intensity.

But I know GOD is behind the "dark cloud," and I know HE will remove the "darkness." I also know this is not a DESTRUCTIVE EXPERIENCE but a CONSTRUCTIVE ONE and that HE is trying to awaken me to a NEW AWARENESS of how to best serve HIM....

HSR

May 22, 1973

Dear "CHASEY,"

Your letter just came, and all I can say is...YOU'RE WONDERFUL! YOU'RE MARVELOUS! YOU'RE INDOMITABLE! YOU'RE INVINCIBLE! YOU'RE INCREDIBLE! But for HEAVEN'S SAKE, KEEP ON BEING "YOU"!

...And I'm not going to say one word about your buying the house. You will always be the IMPULSIVE but BRILLIANT "CHASEY" who jumps in "WHERE ANGELS FEAR TO TREAD"! And I think you are giving your hubby a hard time just watching over you, but I am sure he is smiling through the whole thing and everything will work out great!

...I admire your INDOMITABLE SPIRIT! In fact, I almost ENVY you. It must be wonderful to buy a house with a big yard and two bedrooms and two baths....You'll soon be running a HOTEL, and along with your "AUDUBON TOURS," you'll be entertaining house guests. Again, I say you are INCREDIBLE!!!

As always,

HSR

August 23, 1973

Dear "Chasey,"

...I will not attempt to tell you all the things that have happened to me this summer and are still happening. But through it all what I once believed was a satisfying relationship with GOD has "opened up like a flower in the sun," and I find each hour of the day that I really never knew "THE WONDER OF HIM" for I think I could not live long enough to comprehend it all!

...I could write a lot more, for words say so little WHEN HEARTS MEAN SO MUCH! I can truthfully say that our friendship has been a BRIGHT, BEAUTI-FUL SPOT in my life! Maybe we will get together someday. Of course, we know we will meet "ON THE OTHER SIDE OF DEATH"...and WHAT A HAPPY RE-UNION THAT WILL BE!

Keep enjoying your new home and the luxury of such spaciousness where you can roam around without bumping into yourself!

HSR

September 14, 1973

DEAR, DEAR, DEAR "CHASEY,"

I have only one purpose in writing this note, and that is to put into expression what you already know. And that is to tell you that I will be remembering you especially on your birthday and reliving all the many, many years of our friendship.

...All these things that used to trouble me really trouble me so little now, for the things that seemed the most important have diminished with the years and to just be continuously in a turmoil trying to justify things and settle disputes, is no longer one of my favorite pastimes.

I guess, dear, this will be about the extent of my "conversation" for the present. I'll be writing to you sometime again! Just remember, I think of you as one of the BEST, LITTLE CO-WORKERS who ever came into my life, and I do hope everything is working out fine in your "CACTUS CASTLE"!

HSR

May 2, 1974

DEAR, DEAR "CHASEY,"

I was so very, very glad to get your AIR MAIL LETTER last evening, telling me that you had come home for a little reprieve before they impose the full sentence on you.

Somehow, dear, I just do not seem able to face the situation that is ahead of me. And in these "DARK DAYS of DEEP DISTRESS"...it seems at times LIFE'S A MISERABLE MESS...but that's because I've not GROWN ENOUGH...to really survive when THE GOING IS TOUGH!

But, as you say, YOU ARE MY DEAR COMPANION IN DISCOMFORT...and we will face this thing together...and I am sure we will both somehow survive as we have so many times before!

LOTS of LOVE, dear, and MANY, MANY PRAYERS...Until I feel up to writing more, TAKE CARE!

HSR

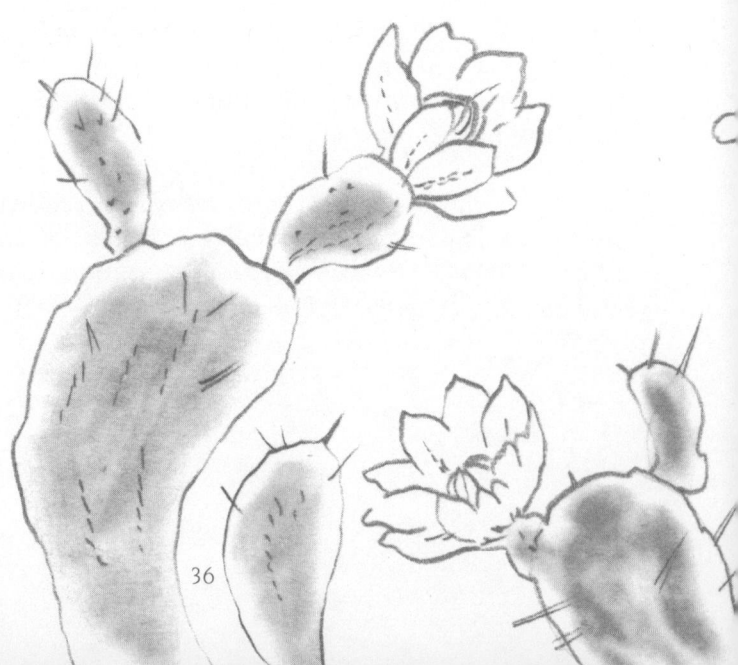

May 29, 1974

DEAR, DEAR "CHASEY,"

With this tumultuous tempest that is threatening me these days, I have lost all track of time. But I just realized that today is the day you are being operated on.

I just want you to know I am "reaching across the miles" with a humble heart that is filled with its own inadequateness, for in these days of soul-agony I realize how pitifully little I ever knew about true humility. Although I have gone through some tragic experiences and thought I had profited by them, I know now I have not even "touched the edge of the FOUNTAIN that holds 'THE LIVING WATER' of GOD!" Now in the agony of my distress, I begin to faintly feel THE JOY of GOD'S BLESSEDNESS...and I just jotted down these words and they really express the way I feel.

> *It's hard for me to understand...the bleakness of my spirit...I tell myself "THY WILL BE DONE"...and I know if I but bow my head...and take what THOU HAST SENT...that I will walk again in the sun...but filled with faith and unafraid...I still feel oddly strange...why can I not be less aware...of the blight that has fallen...and shriveled my soul...when I know so well that YOU CARE...I am content...I do accept...and yet within me rises...an aching hope that I may see...your face not grave and saddened, too...but "smiling" again at me.*

Well, my dear, the laughable part of this whole letter is that YOU ARE THE LADY WHO IS IN THE HOSPITAL WHO NEEDS ENCOURAGEMENT and A "PEP TALK"...and I am burdening you with all my problems! But maybe after all that is good psychology. You'll be so engrossed with my problems, you'll forget about your own problems!

I am relying on you to keep your chin up and to keep smiling.

I hope everything went well and that eventually you, too, like my poor, battered self, will emerge a little STRONGER SPIRITUALLY, so that we are able to meet the next "episode" of life which is ours to endure before we finally reach THE ULTIMATE GOAL we are seeking!

HSR

37

June 18, 1974

CHASEY! CHASEY! CHASEY!

I haven't written, but I know you know that it's true...that I've sure been pray-ing and thinking of you...but I sure don't feel very gay or glib...and this is no time for a "witty ad lib"...so I'm going to write just the way I feel, dear...and let your other friends "dose you daily in cheer."

I think you and I met on "COMMON GROUND"...made "FERTILE" through many years...of UNDERSTANDING FRIENDSHIP..."NURTURED" by LAUGHTER and TEARS...so what can I say to someone who knows...as I know, too...that EVERYTHING is PREORDAINED...and GOD ALWAYS SEES US THROUGH...for we cannot go beyond HIS LOVE...and we're always in HIS CARE...for GOD'S CHILDREN know their FATHER...and their FATHER is with them everywhere!

Now, in a "lighter vein"...If GOD does not have a place ready for you, dear CHASEY, you can depend on HIM to have you "CLIMBING THE CANYONS" and "CUTTING YOUR CACTI" and struggling along with all the rest of us. But just between the two of us, I am still anxiously awaiting for "THE GREEN LIGHT" on "THE KING'S HIGHWAY," for then I can BEGIN to COMMENCE to live in a fuller and better way....

I hope you can read between the lines and know all the love and prayerful wishes that I'm sending you.

HSR

July 29, 1974

Dear "Chasey,"

How pleased I was to get your letter this morning, and how very glad I am that you decided to visit your niece and nephew (who were the BEST THERAPY of all)!

While you know there is a "TIME BOMB TICKING INSIDE OF YOU"...just remember, dear, we all have a "TIME BOMB INSIDE OF US"...only most of us are not aware of it! There really is NO TOMORROW...for TOMORROW is TO-DAY when it arrives...and YESTERDAY is nothing but a MEMORY! So why worry about TOMORROW which may never materialize!

You know, "Chasey," uncertain fear can really depress us. But if we refuse to entertain this, "UNWELCOME GUEST," we save ourselves a lot of agonizing thoughts. However, speaking from experience, THIS IS A DIFFICULT THING TO DO...and nobody knows it better than I do! But I tell myself...LIVE ONLY FOR THE PRESENT MINUTE, FOR ALL ETERNITY IS IN IT!

I can just see you in your LITTLE FRILLY CAP. You are developing an ENTIRE-LY NEW IMAGE!!!??? Instead of "THE LADY WITH THE HAT" (my old name), you have become "THE LADY WITH THE CAP"!

You are really more stylish than I am, for at least you own a wig...and I don't. In this day and age, EVERYBODY who is ANYBODY owns a wig, and I am "certain-sure" that you look real good in your wig. And just like you scorned jewelry at first and then wore it like a QUEEN, so it is with your FRILLY CAPS and your GLAMOUR WIGS. Bet you never knew you would be indulging in all these MODERN BEAUTY AIDS at this stage of the game!

...But you can just bet I'm going to be praying for your complete cure, and I do believe that from now on YOU WILL START TO FEEL BETTER! GOD LOVE YOU, "CHASEY!" YOU ARE A GREAT LITTLE LADY, and I WAS SO HAP-PY TO HEAR FROM YOU!

HSR

September 17, 1974

DEAR, DEAR "CHASEY,"

You've given me a "COMPLEX"...and I DON'T KNOW WHAT TO SAY...I feel RETICENT and TONGUE-TIED...IMAGINE ME THAT WAY?????

You see, you really "shook me up"...with your unforeseen reaction...to my woeful, little missive...that begat dissatisfaction!

So I'll try to be more jolly...and though we're miles apart...I'll concentrate on happy thoughts...when I first laid...my eyes on you...way back in...NINETEEN-THIRTY-TWO...but that might not be good...as you told me to forget..."THE WAY WE WERE"...at the time when we first met...but just between the two of us...I find it kind of pleasant...to get away completely...from "THE MUCH-POLLUTED PRESENT"!

But I can't refrain from saying...in words both TRUE and TERSE...that though "THE GOLDEN YEARS of LIFE"...sound elegant in verse...THEY AIN'T WHAT THEY'RE CRACKED UP TO BE...and who should know better...than AN OLD DAME LIKE ME!

But while growing older has GREAT LIMITATIONS...it makes each CHAPTER in "REVELATIONS"...MORE COMPREHENSIBLE and CLEARER...as THE DAY of JUDGMENT draws just a bit NEARER!...

I certainly hope this finds you in good spirits and enjoying your month's freedom from the "obnoxious treatments."

HSR

November 26, 1974

Dear "CHASEY,"

GOD LOVE YOU, *for I sure do!*

...You know, dear, I'd of just given anything if you could have been sitting in the room with me when I listened to the T.V. broadcast on "DEATH AND DYING" with Dr. Elisabeth Kübler-Ross. I surely agree with everything she said!

"LOVINGLY and PRAYERFULLY"

HSR

P.S. *I'm so glad you decided to postpone those loathsome treatments until af-ter CHRISTMAS. You're a smart gal.*

January 14, 1975

DEAR, DEAR "CHASEY,"

WHAT A SURPRISE TO GET YOUR LETTER. NOTHING ON EARTH COULD HAVE PLEASED ME BETTER.

Like POPCORN in a POPPER...like a SINK without a STOPPER...I am POP-PING with news and OVERFLOWING with chatter...but my office is buzzing and my brains are a scatter...and with hundreds of greetings and "LOVE GIFTS" ga-lore...there isn't an inch of my office floor...that isn't piled high with "TOKENS of LOVE"...and no one except THE GREAT GOD ABOVE...can in any way know how this "tugs at my heart"...and yet I sit here unable to start...but right in the midst of this CHAOTIC STATE...answering your letter's one thing that can't wait...for unless I answer it RIGHT ON THE SPOT...while MY SPIRITS ARE UP and "THE IRON IS HOT"...it will just be placed in "THE MOUNTAIN" of stuff...I will NEVER, NO NEVER, find TIME ENOUGH...to answer in detail WHAT I MOST WANT TO SAY...so that's WHY I'm writing to you TODAY.

...How I wish I could walk into your "CACTUS CASTLE" and just start yakking. There is so much I want to say that I just never could put into a letter.

...I'm very aware that GOD has blessed me, and every day I visit in THE GARDEN OF THE BELOVED and hope that I can be as good a disciple as the one who found THE BELOVED through THE LOVER who worked in GOD'S GARDEN.

I know how blessed I am to have been associated with REVELL, for they are such Christian people. And the paragraph I have marked in the President's last letter to me shows the place that GOD holds in his heart...and his wife is the same kind of a person.

...About the LAETRILLE...I would never discourage you from trying it if you felt moved to give it a whirl. But, personally, I would not go one step to get it myself. I do not think it would hurt you in any way or shorten your length of life on earth, for I feel all our days are numbered by THE DIVINE HAND. And I just push on, working against great odds, secure in the knowledge that, when I have at last come to know HIM as THE ONLY BELOVED ONE, NOTHING CAN EVER HURT ME and I will just go back from whence I came and be part of THE CREATION again. You know, "CHASEY," whether I go to meet HIM TODAY, TOMORROW, or NEXT YEAR is of little consequence to me and it doesn't disturb me at all, for I know man cannot add a day to his life or subtract a day. But if taking this would give you a little lift, I guess even becoming a "smuggler" would not be out of line...and YOU, in many ways, were always "THE DARING ONE."

I think perhaps this will hold you for a little while, and I'll just close as you did, for I like that ending...

> *With much love 'n everything,*
>
> *HSR*

Editor's Note: "Chasey" went to be with the Lord in January 1977. Helen joined her friend on April 23, 1981.

GOD IS LOVE

If people like me
        didn't know people like you
Life would lose its "meaning"
        and its "richness," too
For the friends that we make
        are LIFE's GIFT of LOVE
And I think FRIENDS are
        SENT right from HEAVEN ABOVE
And thinking of you
        somehow makes me feel...
That GOD IS LOVE
        and HE'S VERY REAL

TO "CHASEY"

You'll get a lot of get-well cards
        that say hop out of bed...
But folks who give you that advice
        are crazy in the head...
Why should you hurry and hop out
        and get back on your feet...
It's so much more relaxing when
        you're tucked beneath a sheet...
And the world is such a mess today,
        why, dear, you're right in clover...
IN FACT, I'D LIKE TO JOIN YOU
        IF YOU WOULD JUST MOVE OVER!

FOR A CO-WORKER

For your wisdom and your friendship,
    your counsel and advice,
You've won the admiration
    of Helen Steiner Rice.
And as the years go hurrying by
    I pause and think anew,
How fortunate I was to meet
    a kind, wise friend like you.
I'm but one of many
    who owe a lot to you,
For all the help you've given
    and time and effort too.
And this is just a welcome chance
    to tell you that you've won...
The only REAL SUCCESS in life
    by the FINE THINGS you have done.

FAITH

When the WAY seems long
     And the DAY is DARK,
And we can't hear the song
     Of the thrush or the lark,
And our hearts are heavy
     With worry and care
And we are lost
     in the depths of despair...
That is the time
     when FAITH alone
Can lead us out of
     "THE DARK UNKNOWN,"
For FAITH TO BELIEVE
     when the way is Rough
And FAITH to HANG ON
     when the going is Tough
Will never fail
     to PULL us THROUGH
And bring us
     STRENGTH and COMFORT, too.
For all we really ever need
Is "FAITH AS A GRAIN
     OF MUSTARD SEED"
For all God asks
     is, "Do you believe?"
For if you do
"ye shall receive!"

LIFE IS A GARDEN

Life is a garden,
     Good friends are the flowers,
And times spent together,
     Life's happiest hours;
And friendship, like flowers,
     Blooms ever more fair,
When carefully tended
     By dear friends who care;
And life's lovely garden
     Would be sweeter by far
If all who passed through it
     Were as nice as you are.

FAITH, HOPE, AND LOVE

FAITH...HOPE...and LOVE,
"Three Charms" for your arm,
But each is much more
Than a mere "bracelet charm"—
They are THREE TREASURES
More PRICELESS than GOLD,
For if you possess them
You've riches untold—
For with FAITH to believe
What your eyes cannot see,
And HOPE to look forward
To new joy yet to be,
And LOVE to transform
The most commonplace
Into beauty and kindness
And goodness and grace,
There's NOTHING too MUCH
To accomplish or do,
For with FAITH, HOPE, and LOVE
To carry you through,
Your life will be happy
And full and complete,
For with FAITH, HOPE, and LOVE
The "BITTER" turns "SWEET"—
For all earthly joys
And heaven's joys, too,
Belong to God's children
Who are FAITHFUL and TRUE.

"BEHOLD, I BRING YOU GOOD TIDINGS"

What does this mean to us today...
Just a season that is bright and gay,
A gift...a greeting of good cheer,
The ending of another year?

How little we have understood
The meaning as we really should...
Our minds and hearts have been so small
We never got the real meaning at all!

For in these "TIDINGS" all men received
Much more than they have ever conceived,
For in these words, beyond all seeing,
"WE LIVE AND MOVE AND HAVE OUR BEING."

I SAID A LITTLE PRAYER FOR YOU

I said a little prayer for you
          and I asked the Lord above
To keep you safely in His care
And enfold you in His love
I did not ask for fortune
          for riches or for fame
I only ask for blessings
          in the Saviour's Holy name
Blessings to surround you
in times of trial and stress
And inner joy to fill your heart
          with peace and happiness.

THE WORLD NEEDS
FRIENDLY FOLKS LIKE YOU

In this troubled world
          it's refreshing to find
Someone who still has
          the time to be kind,
Someone who still has
          the faith to believe
That the more you give
          the more you receive,
Someone who's ready
          by thought, word, or deed
To reach out a hand
          in the hour of need.

DISCOURAGEMENT AND DREAMS

So many things in "the line of duty"
Drain us of effort and leave us "no beauty"
And the "dust of the soul" grows thick and unswept
The spirit is drenched in tears unwept
But just as we fall beside the "road"
Discouraged with life and bowed down with our load
We "lift our eyes," and what seemed a "DEAD END"
Is THE STREET OF DREAMS where we meet a FRIEND.

3

Helen, the Poet and the Person

It has been said that the great poet, in writing himself, writes his time. So it was with Helen Steiner Rice. Always honest, forthright, when committed to a cause, her course was straight, her words on target. Her readers know that most of her poems fell into rhyming couplets with stanzas ranging from four lines and sometimes zooming to forty-two.

Less known but perhaps even more impressive are the bits of prose and fiction that came from her pen. Often they were obscured in her personal correspondence. We excerpted one of them for reproduction in this chapter: It is a parable about Jim, a little old tramp and his unflappable, unflagging faith. If when you read it, tears well up in your eyes, you undoubtedly have come to appreciate the delicate balance between the person and the poet, the cause and the concern.

Is there a moral to be drawn from this parable? A lesson to be learned? Let it be a personal one. Helen would have wanted it that way.

Remembering Helen

*P*oetry is generally considered to be cryptic, allusive, hard to understand. So the verse of Helen Steiner Rice is not usually found in literary collections. But her remarkable poems are treasured where it counts — in the hearts of millions of men and women around the world. There is something about her writing reminiscent of the great passages of the Bible — simple and strong and true. No wonder so many people who would never buy a book of "poetry" love the lilting lines of Helen Steiner Rice.

It is not by accident that the word love appears in the titles of so many of the books of Helen Steiner Rice. She was a woman of amazing love. She gave of herself not only in the singing words that have made her famous, but in many ways. On reading her poems, thousands of people were moved to write to her. And Helen insisted on replying personally to great numbers of such individuals.

Her verse is not just pleasant words. It represents her deepest convictions — her sturdy faith and her upbeat philosophy. She knew that every end of the road was just a bend in the road, every stranger a friend one hasn't met, every busy thoroughfare a place to meet angels unawares.

Donald T. Kauffman
Former Managing Editor,
Fleming H. Revell Company
Coauthor of Love and
Mothers Are a Gift of Love

Dear C —

I have gotten a lot of "soul-satisfaction" out of an experience I had at church recently. We have a Praise God Shared Service before the minister starts his preaching. I told the little story of the tramp who daily went to the large magnificent cathedral. To the consternation of the sexton, the tramp would kneel at the altar for just a minute and then leave. Then one day the sexton told him never to come back again, because he knew he was not up to any good. The poor little fellow was completely crushed, and he said, "I only come here to pray," and the sexton replied, "You only stay a minute and nobody can pray to GOD in a second!" The tramp said, "I don't know many words, but JESUS understands, for all I say is 'JESUS, it's Jim, and HE always says, 'Hello, Jim,' and then I go." But the sexton was not moved, and he forbid him to ever return.

As the little old man crossed the street, he was struck by an automobile, which disabled him completely. He was taken to the hospital ward and thrown in with a lot of derelicts and bums who did nothing but complain and swear. But after he had been in the ward for several months, the nurse noticed that the men no longer swore, and they seemed to have a completely different attitude. Asking how this could have happened to all of them, they said, "It's that little old man in such great pain who never complains and always has that beautiful smile on his face!"

So the nurse went over to Jim's bed, and she told him, "Jim, you have had a marvelous influence on these men, but I don't understand how you can be spiritually at peace when you are physically in such pain." He said, "Well, it's my VISITOR!" But she knew that he had never had a visitor, and she said, "I've never seen a visitor here...When does your visitor come?" He replied, "HE comes daily at noon, and HE stands at the foot of my bed and HE says, 'Jim, this is JESUS,' and then I feel after I have seen HIM that nothing in the world can hurt me." Then, looking up with a smile on his face, he said, "Just think HE comes to see me because HE knows I can't go to see HIM anymore!"

HSR

DISAPPOINTMENT

It's hard to explain—this feeling of woe,
     That enwraps every part of our being
It's hard to interpret the sadness and hurt
     That keeps us the sunlight from seeing.

The world looks so dreary—so cold and so dull
     There isn't a thing to enjoy,
I wonder why we must experience this grief
     Why happiness it does destroy?

Just an aching and breaking, a hurt and a pain
     That comes from an action or word,
A longing, a gnawing, a feeling of loss
     The depth of this sorrow's unheard.

And yet if we had no sorrows
     How valueless joy would be,
For we never could know the depth and height
     Of triumph and victory!
          HES

THE CENTER OF THE FLAME

In the center of the flame
    there is a hollow place
And nothing can burn
    in this sheltered space
For the fire builds a wall
    scientific fact claims
And insures a safe area
    in the midst of the flames
And in the hurricane's fury
    there's a center of peace
Where the winds of destruction
    suddenly cease
And this same truth prevails
    in life's tribulations
There's an island of calm
    in the soul's meditations
A place that is quiet
    where we're shielded from harms
Secure in the haven
    of a kind Father's arms
Where the hot flames of anger
    have no power to sear
And the high winds of hatred
    and violence and fear
Lose all the wrath
    of their savage course
And are softly subdued
    as FAITH weakens FORCE
So when the fires of life
    burn deep in your heart
And the winds of destruction
    seem to tear you apart
Remember God loves you
    and wants to protect you
So seek that small haven
    and be guided by prayer
To that place of protection
    within God's loving care.

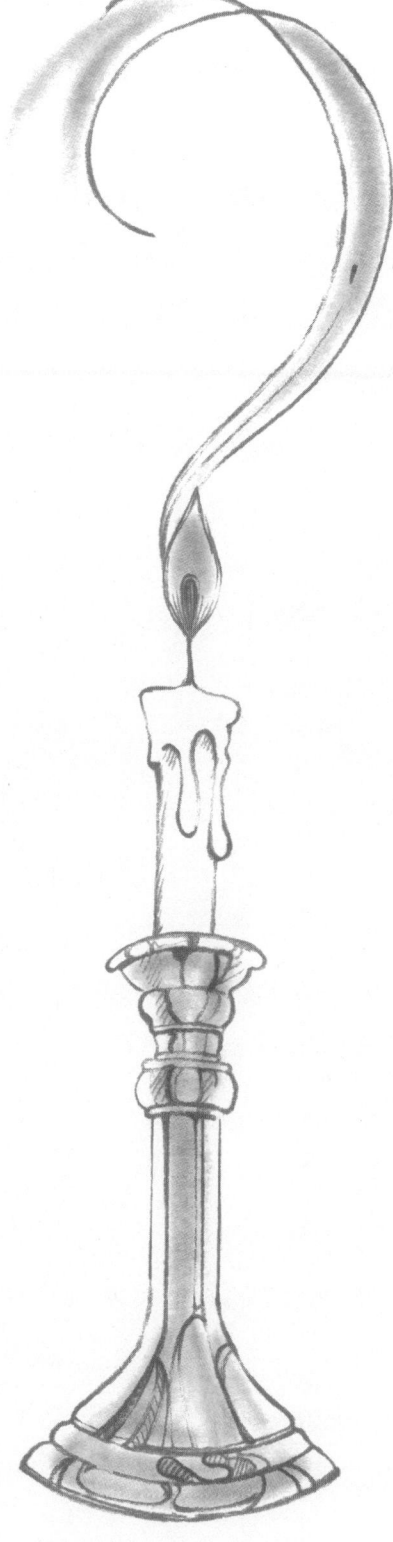

SMILE

When you DO what you DO
      with a WILL and a SMILE....

Everything that you DO will seem
      TWICE as WORTHWHILE....

And when you walk down the street,
      life will seem TWICE as SWEET

If you SMILE at the people
      you happen to meet....

For when you SMILE it is true
      folks will SMILE back at you....

So DO what you DO
      with a WILL and a SMILE

And WHATEVER YOU DO
      WILL BE TWICE as WORTHWHILE.

A PRAYER FOR SERENITY

GOD, be MY RESTING PLACE and MY PROTECTION
IN HOURS of TROUBLE, DEFEAT, and REJECTION...
May I never give way to SELF-PITY and SORROW,
May I always BE SURE of a BETTER TOMORROW.
May I stand undaunted COME WHAT MAY,
SECURE IN THE KNOWLEDGE I HAVE ONLY TO PRAY
And ASK MY CREATOR and FATHER ABOVE
TO KEEP ME SERENE in HIS GRACE and HIS LOVE!

TIME FOR A TUNE-UP

When your "axle" is a-draggin'
      and your "tires" are wearin' thin,

Then birthdays aren't something
      that you welcome with a grin.

And I'm speaking from experience,
      although it's sad but true,

FATHER TIME and MOTHER NATURE
      sure can make it tough for you.

I'll admit I'm getting mildewed
      and my carburetor's busted,

My chassis's cracked and dented,
      and my spark plugs all are rusted.

But what's the use of griping
      because you've stripped your gears,

You can't expect to feel like TWENTY
      when you've lived for FIFTY YEARS.

WE ARE THE "GO-GO" GENERATION

We are not old-fashioned or outdated squares
We are the true "GO-GO'S" with which nothing compares.
We are following instructions received centuries ago
When Christ spoke these words, "AS MY WORKERS, NOW GO,"
GO into the world with its evil and sin
GO in My Name and GO out to win
To all who are seeking a haven of truth
GO tell the story to the lonely, lost youth
GO make them your friends and share this great joy
For this is the inheritance God gave each girl and boy
GO not tomorrow but start out today
To fill God's great vision of the true GO-GO way
Have fun in the going, for there's joy yet unknown
And the best of it all is you don't go alone.

THERE'S ALWAYS A TIME

There's a TIME to be BORN
          and a TIME to DIE,
A TIME to LAUGH
          and a TIME to CRY,
A TIME to RUN
          and a TIME to go SLOW,
A TIME to STOP
and a TIME to GO—
And a TIME to BEGIN
and a TIME to QUIT,
And something tells me
that THIS is "IT"!

THE WINDOWS OF GOLD

There is a legend that has often been told
Of the boy who searched for THE WIN-
        DOWS OF GOLD,
The beautiful windows he saw far away
When he looked in the valley at sunrise
        each day,
And he yearned to go down to the valley
        below
But he lived on a mountain that was cov-
        ered with snow
And he knew it would be a difficult trek,
But that was a journey he wanted to
        make,
So he planned by day and he dreamed
        by night
Of how he could reach THE GREAT
        SHINING LIGHT...
And one golden morning when dawn
        broke through
And the valley sparkled with diamonds
        of dew
He started to climb down the mountain-
        side
With THE WINDOWS OF GOLD as his
        goal and his guide...
He traveled all day and, weary and worn,
With bleeding feet and clothes that were
        torn
He entered the peaceful valley town
Just as the golden sun went down...
But he seemed to have lost his "GUID-
        ING LIGHT,"
The windows were dark that had once
        been bright,
And hungry and tired and lonely and
        cold
He cried, "WON'T YOU SHOW ME THE
        WINDOWS OF GOLD?"
And a kind hand touched him and
        said, "BEHOLD, HIGH ON THE
MOUNTAIN ARE THE WINDOWS
        OF GOLD"—

For the sun going down in a great golden
	ball
Had burnished the windows of his cabin
	so small,
And THE KINGDOM OF GOD with its
	GREAT SHINING LIGHT,
Like the Golden Windows that shone so
	bright,
Is not a far distant place somewhere,
It's as close to you as a silent prayer—
And your search for God will end and
	begin
When you look for HIM and FIND HIM
	WITHIN.

4

Helen, the Comforter

*L*ike a precious, sparkling jewel, the life of Helen Steiner Rice had many facets. Perhaps one which shone more brilliantly than all of the others was that which reflected her as comforter to the bereaved.

Helen was well acquainted with that condition of the body and the spirit. As a teenager, she suffered the loss of her dear father; as a bride she was confronted with the untimely death of her husband of two years. Excerpts from her correspondence dated January 1969 constitute the "Remembering" section of this chapter and reflect on the dark days following Franklin's death.

Sympathy and empathy were words she understood deeply and characteristics she personified completely. Perhaps this is best illustrated in the letter that appears in this chapter. It was written in response to the request from a friend whose sister was deeply in the throes of despair: her beautiful daughter had been murdered on Easter Sunday and she was unable to cope with that grim, heartbreaking reality.

Remembering

...There are indeed many things in life that we cannot understand, but we must trust God's judgment and be guided by His hand. And every day I find new evidence that nothing in life is by "CHANCE or HAPPENSTANCE" but by "DIVINE DESIGN." Things that baffled me for many, many years suddenly become "crystal clear," and I can see where what I thought was "an unbearable tragedy" was "a gift from God" that added new dimensions to my life and widened my vision.

...It took me over thirty years to completely understand Franklin's "sudden departure" from my life and this world. But now I look at his picture, and I can tell him that his desire was fulfilled...for in his last note his one concern was that he could not give me all the luxuries that money can buy as he had so wanted.

But his "going out" was my "coming in," and he made it possible for me to write these little poems which seem to have reached the hearts of people all around the world. I know now that you can never "dry another's tears" unless you, too, have "wept." And I say again nothing but the hand of God, shaping my life over a "DIVINE PATTERN," could have had things turn out the way they did....

HSR

Dear V —

I've never met you, it's true...but I know your sister, so I feel I know you, too...and with GOD there are no strangers, so although we're miles apart...HE will draw us all together and unite us in SPIRIT and HEART!

R — told me of the tragedy that has torn your heart apart. There's so little words can say to soften your sorrow, for it's so overwhelming that you are lost in the agony and the anguish of its immensity.

But Sunday will be Mother's Day, and I am hoping that through remembrance you will gain strength to realize that the purpose of all living is to die and that death just "OPENS THE DOOR TO THE GLORY OF LIVING." And I can promise you, dear, that your daughter is waiting to welcome you in that place where time is not counted by years and there are no separations!

I know all these words seem very meaningless to you now. But I am only going to ask you one thing, and that is to think of the wonderful years you experienced as B's mother. In doing this, it will awaken THE MIRACLE of her BIRTH. And if you dwell on this thought and all the joy she brought, you will understand that, just as GOD gave this baby girl to you and did not lose her in the giving, you have not lost her in returning her to GOD, who only loaned her to you for a little while.

BIRTH and DEATH in GOD'S HANDS are still unfathomable mysteries. When B — was born into this world, it was GOD who breathed the breath of life into her. While man has figured out the process of conception and birth, it was GOD, and GOD ALONE, who breathed life into what was physically conceived, and it will always remain the secret that only ETERNITY can unveil. And she has just "burst her chrysalis of clay" and "winged her way" into THE LIGHT OF ETERNAL DAY.

WHY this tragedy should be, we all ask, and we cannot help but wonder how this KIND, WONDERFUL GOD could allow this brutal violence to happen to this lovely, innocent girl. But GOD had taken care of all this by lifting her soul out of her body before death was even apparent to her.

And you must never think of death being sent as punishment, for even if it comes in this cruel, inhuman way, GOD did not send it. Violence is only the product of man, for GOD gives us all a choice. But the majority of mankind prefers to live in a violent world of sex, sin, speed, greed and ungodliness. It was man himself who changed all GOD'S plans, and now GOD'S CHILDREN are the innocent victims of sinful mankind.

However, this does not mean that GOD is not with them and taking care of them, for, Dear, our lives are more than a PHYSICAL JOURNEY. It is supposed to be a SPIRITUAL EXPERIENCE, for only through great suffering and sorrow can we come to know what GOD is really like, and inner strength can only be gained from deep sorrow and suffering.

While it is difficult to accept this, we know GOD never makes mistakes and HE never "plows in a field" that HE does not intend to "sow with seeds." And when HE "sows SPIRITUAL SEEDS," there's always a "crop" to fill "THE STORE-HOUSE OF THE SOUL" to "overflowing"!

If you recall, it says in THE BIBLE, "They meant it for evil, but GOD meant it for good!" There are many times when injustice seems to be dominant, and it is only natural to feel GOD'S LAW of JUSTICE is not always at work. But GOD'S LAW will adjust and regulate all kinds of conditions and situations. So, I'm going to ask you to keep praying without ceasing, and remember WHATSOEVER YOU WILL ASK IN PRAYER, THAT YOU WILL RECEIVE if you truly love THE LORD and are looking forward to dwelling with HIM someday.

R — said she sent you my book, LIFE IS FOREVER. And when the stabbing pain and overwhelming grief has lessened, you will find comfort and consolation in knowing GOD lifted your daughter gently into a place where she is safe and free and she waits for you in ETERNITY.

Until you are once again able to stand on your own strength, you will have to just borrow strength from GOD and let a prayer be your STANDING GROUND.

So, take THE SAVIOUR'S LOVING HAND...and DO NOT TRY TO UNDER-STAND...just let HIM lead you where HE will...through "pastures green and waters still"...and place yourself in HIS LOVING CARE...and HE will gladly help you bear...whatever lies ahead of you...and GOD will see you SAFELY THROUGH...and no earthly pain is ever too much...if GOD bestows HIS MER-CIFUL TOUCH!

So, I commend you into HIS CARE...with a loving thought and a SPECIAL PRAYER...and always remember, WHATEVER BETIDE YOU...GOD IS AL-WAYS BESIDE YOU...and you cannot go beyond GOD'S REACH or beyond HIS LOVE and CARE...for we are all a PART of GOD, and GOD is EVERYWHERE!

"LOVINGLY and PRAYERFULLY,"

HSR

TO FRANKLIN

In my eyes there lies no vision
But the sight of your dear face,
In my heart there is no feeling
But the warmth of your embrace
In my mind there are no thoughts
But the thoughts of you, my dear
In my soul no other longing
But just to have you near
All my dreams are built around you
And I've come to know it's true
In my life there is no living
That is not a part of YOU.

DEATH CLOSES ONE DOOR
AND OPENS ANOTHER

Death is just a natural thing,
     like the closing of a door,
As we start upon a journey
     to a new and distant shore.
So let your grief be softened
     and yield not to despair
You have only placed your loved one
     in the loving Father's care.

SINCE MOTHER WENT AWAY

Since Mother went away, it seems
She's nearer than before—
I cannot touch her hand and yet
She's with me more and more....
And years have never lessened
The longing in my heart
That came the day I realized
That we must dwell apart—
And just as long as memory lives
My Mother cannot die,
For in my heart she's living still,
As passing years go by.

THE HOME BEYOND

We are so sad
        when those we love
Are called to live
        in that HOME ABOVE,
But why should we grieve
        when they say good-bye
And go to dwell
        in a "cloudless sky,"
For they have but gone
        to prepare the way
And we'll join them again
        some happy day.

THE SOUL, LIKE NATURE, HAS SEASONS, TOO

When you feel cast down and despondently sad
And you long to be happy and carefree and glad,
Do you ask yourself, as I so often do,
Why must there be days that are cheerless and blue?
Why is the song silenced in the heart that was gay?
And then I ask God, "What Makes Life This Way?"
And His explanation makes everything clear,
The Soul Has Its Seasons the same as the year,
Man, too, must pass through life's Autumn of death
And have his heart frozen by Winter's cold breath—
But Spring always comes with new life and birth
Followed by Summer to warm the soft earth—
And, oh, what a comfort to know there are reasons
That souls, like Nature, must too have their seasons,
Bounteous Seasons and Barren Ones, too,
Times For Rejoicing and Times To Be Blue—
For with nothing but "Sameness" how dull life would be
For only life's challenge can set the soul free,
And it takes a mixture of both Bitter and Sweet
To Season our Lives and make them complete.

THE PROMISE OF HEAVEN

I know how you'll feel
        when the Christmas bells ring,
But here is a thought
        to which you can cling...
This is the birthday
        of Jesus whose love
Assures you of meeting
        your loved ones above...
And this glorious story
        of our Saviour's birth
Is our promise of heaven
        after this earth.

HE'S ONLY GONE ON

At last his gallant soul
    "TOOK FLIGHT"
Into the "LAND
    WHERE THERE IS NO NIGHT"...
But his name is CARVED
    in OUR HEARTS to stay
As we think of the things
    that he used to say...
So he is not dead,
    he's only "GONE ON"
Into a "BRIGHTER,
    MORE WONDERFUL DAWN"...
For men like him
    were not born to die
But, like the SUN
    that shines in the SKY,
They warm the "earth"
    and the "hearts of men"
And in HAPPY REMEMBRANCE
    they live again...
So while he sleeps
    and his voice is still,
His spirit goes on
    and it always will.

STEPPINGSTONES TO GOD

An aching heart is but a steppingstone
      To greater joy than you've ever known
For things that cause the heart to ache
Until you feel that it must break
Become strength by which we climb
To higher heights that are sublime
The grace to soar above life's trials
And feel the radiance of God's smiles
So when you're overwhelmed with fears
And all your hopes are drenched in tears
Think not that life has been unfair
And given you too much to bear....
For God has chosen you because
With all your weaknesses and flaws
HE feels that you are worthy of
THE GREATNESS of HIS WONDROUS LOVE
So welcome every stumbling block
And every thorn and jagged rock
For each one is a STEPPINGSTONE
To GOD, who wants YOU for HIS OWN
For discipline in daily duty
Will shape your life for deeper beauty
And as you grow in strength and grace
The clearer you can see GOD'S FACE
And on the STEPPINGSTONES of STRIFE
YOU reach at last ETERNAL LIFE.

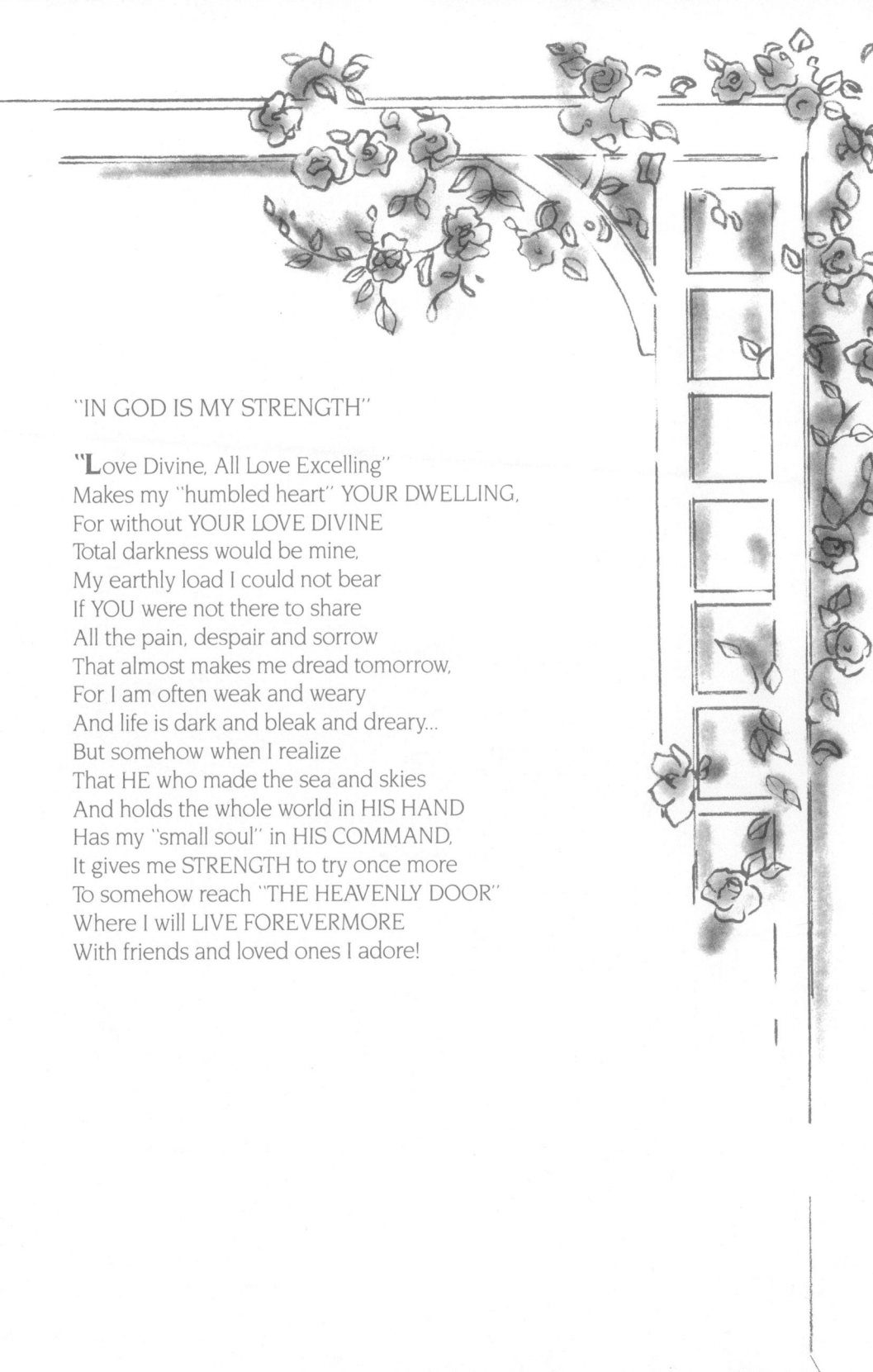

"IN GOD IS MY STRENGTH"

"Love Divine, All Love Excelling"
Makes my "humbled heart" YOUR DWELLING,
For without YOUR LOVE DIVINE
Total darkness would be mine,
My earthly load I could not bear
If YOU were not there to share
All the pain, despair and sorrow
That almost makes me dread tomorrow,
For I am often weak and weary
And life is dark and bleak and dreary...
But somehow when I realize
That HE who made the sea and skies
And holds the whole world in HIS HAND
Has my "small soul" in HIS COMMAND,
It gives me STRENGTH to try once more
To somehow reach "THE HEAVENLY DOOR"
Where I will LIVE FOREVERMORE
With friends and loved ones I adore!

GOD'S PLAN

And although it sometimes seems to us
        Our prayers have not been heard,
God always knows our every need
        Without a single word...
And He will not forsake us
        Even though the way seems steep,
For always He is near to us—
        A tender watch to keep...
And in good time He'll answer us
        And in His love He'll send
GREATER THINGS THAN WE HAVE ASKED
        And blessings without end...
So though we do not understand
        Why trouble comes to man
Can we not be contented
        Just to know THAT IT'S GOD'S PLAN?

THERE IS NO DEATH

There is no night without a dawning,
No Winter without a Spring,
And beyond death's dark horizon
Our hearts once more will sing—
For those who leave us for a while
Have only GONE AWAY
Out of a restless, careworn world
Into a "BRIGHTER DAY"
Where there will be no partings
And time is not counted by years,
Where there are no trials or troubles,
No worries, no cares and no tears.

AS LONG AS YOU LIVE AND REMEMBER—
YOUR LOVED ONE LIVES IN YOUR HEART!

May tender memories
  soften your grief,
May fond recollection
  bring you relief,
And may you find comfort
  and peace in the thought
Of the joy that knowing
  your loved one brought—
For time and space
  can never divide
Or keep your loved one
  from your side
When memory paints
  in colors true
The happy hours
  that belonged to you.

DEATH IS A GATEWAY

We feel so sad when those we love
Are touched by death's dark hand,
But it would ease our sorrow
If we could but understand
That death is just a gateway
That all men must pass through
And on the other side of death,
In a world that's bright and new,
Our loved ones wait to welcome us
To that land free from all tears
Where joy becomes eternal
And time is not counted by years.

5

Helen, the Businesswoman

Helen Steiner Rice was the consummate businesswoman.

She was a goal setter—and keeper.

She was an all-giving person.

She championed the little man when he was right, and she argued against the big man when he wasn't, corporations and government notwithstanding. The story is told that when one of the women in her company was fired—Helen believed unjustly—the following day she stood in silent protest, reading her Bible as the employees filed into work.

Her attention to detail was meticulous, her dedication unwavering in the production of the total product.

By her own admission she was not a feminist in the twenties or during any of the decades that followed. But she did indeed enlighten views on women in business. She thought it was "stupid and wasteful" to overlook women in job promotion because of sex. She believed them to be ambitious, industrious, patient, dependable, friendly, adaptable, tactful, cheerful, neat, and intuitive. This last talent was especially valued: "I have seen women in business draw on intuition to make a tough decision, and more often than not their instincts proved correct."

The "Lorain Tornado," as she was known early in her career, made it the hard way from the age of eighteen through her eightieth year. And while she, of necessity, chose the role of the working woman, the businesswoman, she never eschewed, scored, or berated the woman who was not career-minded. She had reverence for her: "The best things are nearest: breath in your nostrils, light in your eyes, flowers at your feet, duties at your hand, the path of Right just before you. Then do not grasp at the stars, but do life's plain, common work as it comes, certain that daily duties and daily bread are the sweetest things of life."

THURSDAY OCT 18

Remembering Helen

*K*nown as the "middleman" between author and reader, the book publisher plays a significant role in the communication of ideas. *The publisher of Christian books is especially privileged, I believe, because he and his co-workers have a real commitment: the publication of writings that reach through the minds to the* hearts *of readers.*

First in the publishing process, publisher and author draw up and agree to what is known as the publishing contract. Then with a real empathy for the author's subject and message, the publisher assists in the editorial phase of the project. Finally, with the manuscript completed, the publisher endeavors to manufacture and market a book worthy of the author's material.

Among the scores of authors with whom Wilbur H. Davies, longtime president of Fleming H. Revell Company, and I had contact, I have special and fond recollections of working closely with Helen Steiner Rice, year after year, through every phase of the publication of twenty-four different editions of "HSR" books.

"The Lord gives me these verses to share with others," she so often said. And once the verse was placed on paper, Helen became an integral part of the publication process—selection of verses, always with a focus: Love, Mother, Death, Friendship; number of verses and amount of artwork to be included; title; design of jacket...and, finally, the overall appearance of the completed product, Yes, Helen was a perfectionist, involved each step of the way until the book was completed. "Now God will take charge of the book from this point on." And indeed He did! Millions of copies of HSR books have been, and are being, purchased, given, read, and treasured by Christians and non-Christians around the globe.

Helen was firm in her own personal relationship with God and equally firm in seeing her writings as truly a ministry-in-print. During each business meeting with her publisher—in her office, her hotel, her apartment—Helen Steiner Rice had a time for praise and prayer. "Thank You, Lord, thank You. Now help us, guide us...."

> William R. Barbour, Jr.
> Past Chairman,
> Fleming H. Revell Company

Editor's Note: The fundamental characteristics Helen espoused in 1924 remained important to her throughout her life, as indicated in this letter of recommendation.

July 23, 1975

Dear Mr. —

...In this world of casual carelessness and impudent indifference, how fortunate for the employer to find a dedicated, delightful, happy, honorable, intelligent, and interested employee who is endowed with high ideals, effervescent enthusiasm, and who is pretty and polite in the bargain!

I know there are many charts and standards for the evaluation of "CHARACTER." But I am just old-fashioned enough to be impressed by truth, honesty, integrity, and ideals, and this young lady, L —, is certainly MY INTERPRETATION of "CHARACTER."

I understand that you are a comparatively new Company that is eagerly enthusiastic about their product and that you are a privately owned Corporation and not a power-mad conglomerate. In my estimation, these huge conglomerates are "the root of all evil" in our commercial world today.

May I wish you GOOD LUCK in all your endeavors!

HSR

Editor's Note: In 1924 Helen Elaine Steiner was Manager of Advertising for the Ohio Public Service Company in Lorain, Ohio. She was also serving as Ohio State Chairman of the Women's Public Information Committee, N.E.L.A. She had written and had published a prize-winning article on public relations in Forbes Magazine. Her talent as a public speaker and motivator was beginning to be discovered, and across the country the demand for her appearance at sales meetings and banquets was growing by leaps and bounds. During that year, she contributed several articles to the Chicago-based magazine, Electric Light and Power, *that represented the industry. We have chosen two excerpts from the articles because they represent what a forward-thinking young woman she was.*

BITS TO REMEMBER

Be Cheerful, Courteous, Considerate and Co-operate at all times.

Maintain good business principles and an attractive business house — always.

Resolve that the business of selling is just as legitimate as the business of buying.

Study Human Nature in Selling.

Keep a good accounting system — for accurate figures always show the Weak Spots in business, almost unerringly. It is by the means of these figures that you are able to observe business tendencies and take full advantage of their significance.

Bear in mind that annual profit falls when larger stocks accumulate and when accounts receivable are not collected promptly — when expenses increase and gross margin is reduced.

Constant Vigilance in business is rewarded by profit.

While Overhead plays a big part in deciding the annual net profit, Turnover plays a far more important role.

Conform to the Golden Rule and continue "To Profit Most as You Serve Best."

From "A Good Story of Constructive Merchandising," May 1924

90

PERMIT me to elaborate on the fundamental characteristics inherent in women which particularly fit them for the developing and maintaining of sound public relations. It is only voicing the obvious to say: "To do a thing for a customer is to do it for your own company." Goodwill brings into our business that which we could never hope to obtain as a "monopoly." Women have the power within them to create goodwill, by these traits emphasized in their sex:

(1). Women have ambition to succeed: Generally speaking, they have the will and the desire to improve their minds....they have not merely a vague, intermittent desire for knowledge, but a real longing and earnest will to succeed.

(2). Women are usually very industrious: They have the ability to drive themselves steadily — accomplishing in certain kinds of duties more work, in a more accurate way, than their masculine co-workers. Women are conscientious — a fair promise of faithful performance of the task.

(3). Women are patient: It has even been conceded that they are doubly blessed with this attribute and in so being they are enabled to take care of people, of varying dispositions and with a diversity of grievances, eight hours a day and three hundred and sixty-five days a year and not have their temper fray at the edges.

(4). Women are dependable: They can be relied upon to carry out plans assigned to them; the fault today is that enough important work is not delegated to them. Women as a whole are proud of any trust placed in them by their employers and try with increased zeal to prove that confidence has not been misplaced.

(5). Women are friendly: They have a way of gaining confidences easily. A woman's viewpoint and friendliness is always of value and even an actual necessity is selling appliances. They have a keener knowledge of women and their problems and can sell to them with a clearer understanding.

(6). Women possess adaptability: They find it easy to listen to what their customers are saying. They can get the other person's viewpoint and they can put themselves in the customer's place.

(7). Women have tact: They work in harmony with other people. They are capable of weighing the claims, wishes and demands of the public in the scales of good judgment and tactfully arriving at a satisfactory agreement to all concerned.

(8). Women radiate cheerfulness: They take an enthusiastic interest in the affairs of their customers; they are not cold or unresponsive to complaints registered by the public, real or imaginary — and, remember, imaginary grievances sometimes cause more havoc than real ones.

I have confident belief that only a more general acceptance of the fact that women should be given a definite place, not through courtesy, but by the necessities of work to be done for which they are especially well fitted, is needed to take down completely and permanently the bars of sex prejudice.

From "Women Have Won Greater Opportunity," December 1924

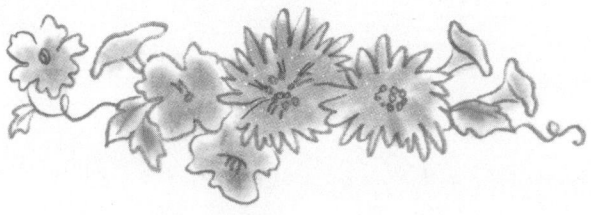

IN BUSINESS AND IN LIFE
THE SAME RULES APPLY
AND THE "TEN COMMANDMENTS"
ARE THE BEST TO LIVE BY.

WHO DO YOU WORK FOR?

I work for God and I work for His glory
In all that I do I retell the old story
The story of life and how we should live
How we should share and continuously give.

A PRAYER

Oh Lord don't let me falter
Don't let me lose my way
Don't let me cease to carry
My burden day by day.

Oh Lord don't let me stumble
Don't let me fall and quit
Oh Lord please help me find my job
And help me shoulder it.

TO OUR FAVORITE WAITRESS

Now, every day we fellows meet,
Because it seems that man must eat,
So every noon we congregate
To eat the "Special luncheon plate."
And while the food we get is good
We want it strictly understood,
That "stew" and "hash" can taste like "pheasant"
When being SERVED by SOMEONE PLEASANT.
And we will never "gripe" or "fuss"
As long as YOU will wait on us.
For you add "APPETITE APPEAL"
To every mouthful of our meal.
So here's a little CHRISTMAS CASH
For the GIRL WHO GLORIFIES our HASH!

A PRAYER
Written Especially for
THE CHINA PAINTERS' CONVENTION
May 16, 1969

God, as we gather here today
        from many different places,
Grant us warmth and friendliness
        and happy smiling faces
So everybody gathered here
        will not feel STRANGE or NEW
But like "OLD FRIENDS" just meeting
        to discuss the work they do—
And may we learn a lot of things
        about color and design,
But may we also take away
        some things that are divine—
The knowledge that we all need love,
        for a full, rich life depends
Not on success or worldly fame
        but in sharing with our friends
Some happy, little hobby,
        some talent, skill or art,
Or just some new ideas
        or kindred thoughts of heart—
So, bless this "confederation"
        in its "pursuit of beauty,"
For the choicest china painting
        is done for love not duty,
And when this meeting's over
        may fond memories remain
To keep alive the friendships
        we made while in Lorain.

MEET THE SUCCESS FAMILY

Would you like an introduction
To the FAMILY of SUCCESS?
Would you like to form a friendship
That would lead to happiness?
Would you like to meet the "FATHER"
And the "SONS" and "DAUGHTERS" too?
Would you like to know the "MOTHER"
And have the "BABY" smile on you?

Well, meet the FATHER—he is WORK;
The MOTHER is AMBITION;
The CHILDREN are a source of pride,
They uphold the best tradition;
The oldest "SON" is COMMON SENSE,
PERSEVERANCE is his BROTHER,
While HONESTY and FORESIGHT
Are "TWINS" to one another;
The DAUGHTER's name is CHARACTER,

Her SISTERS' names are CHEER
And LOYALTY and COURTESY
And PURPOSE that's SINCERE:
The BABY of the FAMILY
Is mighty "SWEET" to know,
Its name is OPPORTUNITY,
You'll want to see it grow;
And if you get acquainted
With the FATHER you will find
The members of HIS FAMILY
Are just the nicest kind;
And if you form a FRIENDSHIP
With the FAMILY of SUCCESS
You'll get an introduction
To the HOUSE of HAPPINESS.

NEW CONCEPTS AND OLD COMMANDMENTS

Even in business there are COMMANDMENTS to OBEY,
Little daily disciplines we must practice every day.
We must always have before us an OBJECTIVE and a GOAL,
Just as each man must make a plan for his eternal soul,
And we must learn in business to readily ADJUST,
And to study "BEING HUMAN" is a necessary MUST.
For business management concedes, without any disagreeing,
The greatest asset they possess is MAN, "THE HUMAN BEING."
For with all our growth and progress in science and machines
And all our skill and "know-how" and fabulous routines,
We still are merely robots unless by grace we find
That the HEART of MAN is GREATER than his quick computing mind.
So let us all remember as we pursue our course,
In every situation we win by FAITH and NOT BY FORCE,
And all our great achievements, our knowledge and our skill
Are SUBJECT and SUBSERVIENT to THE HOLY FATHER'S WILL!

LIFE

If you would aspire a salesman to be
The rulings are simple and few;
Just work, be happy, and never forget
You're paid for whatever you do.

If you bargain with Life for a penny—
You'll find Life will pay you no more,
And you'll feel that you've failed completely
When you figure your final score.

If you realize Life's an employer
That pays you whatever you ask,
You'll learn to be honest and never deceive
In any performance or task.

So just set your wage at the highest stake,
And never give up in dismay,
For any wage you may ask of Life,
Old "Life" will so gladly pay.
                    HES

6

Helen, the Environmentalist and the Patriot

The setting sun, the sparkle of a raindrop, a flower's scent, the iridescence of a snowflake, these and other phenomena of nature never escaped the watchful and discerning eye of Helen Steiner Rice.

She was also an astute observer of man in his pursuits—humane, business, political, and patriotic. When she believed in a cause, she championed it. Her pen became her sword and she brandished it with conviction.

She was a woman for all seasons, a purveyor of dreams and righteousness. And a protector of them.

Remembering Helen

I grew up in an era — happily not forgotten — when someone quite close but not a family member was called "Aunt" or "Uncle." Helen Steiner Rice was "Aunt Helen" as long as I can remember. Aunt Helen's warmth and cheerfulness were reflected not just in her writings — and in her colorful and somewhat bizarre hats — but in her view of the world. She truly loved all of God's creatures, found happiness and harmony in nature, loved flowers and trees, and saw the seasons change with a mixture of awe and gratitude. Awe at the beauty of the Lord's handiwork. Gratitude for the privilege of glimpsing immortality through the immutable laws of the universe. She was an environmentalist in the best sense, treasuring the gifts that are our common heritage and make up the world around us, and wanting to pass these on untouched to generations yet unborn. When I visited Aunt Helen in the quiet of the nursing home where she spent her last days, the spark of her lively mind, keen memory, and concern for others was always there, despite frailty and pain. And in that setting — unable to move about outside — she never failed to show reverence for the treasures around us which she could only enjoy through the window of her room.

Willis D. Gradison
United States Representative
Ohio

May 22, 1973

Dear —

...I don't know how you feel about WATERGATE, but I feel our whole society is structured on manipulation, intrigue, conspiracy, and complicity, and the majority of people operating in this world today are COUNTERFEITS without even recognizing how pitifully PHONY they are. To me, WATERGATE is not only a POLITICAL PROBLEM, but it is a PERSONAL PART of our EVERY-DAY LIVING!

But when I look back and think of Pilate and Herod in the days of JESUS, I know they had their ANCIENT WATERGATES. So life goes on, and MEN NEVER LEARN....

HSR

Dear C —

...I am working on a new poem, which I probably will never finish, but I feel so deeply that man has built his own "HELL" on earth! "He took the good earth and 'the fulness thereof'...which GOD gave to him as a GIFT of HIS LOVE...and he polluted the air and ravished the sod...and completely destroyed the good earth of GOD...he cut down the forests with ruthless disdain...and the earth's natural beauty he perverted for gain...he has made of himself a GIANT of GREED...in a world where the PASSWORD is SEX, SIN, and SPEED...and now in an age filled with violent dissent...he finds he's imprisoned in his own discontent...and what GOD created to be man's paradise...became through man's lust, perversion, and vice...a CALDRON of CHAOS in a FOG of POLLUTION...to which man can find NO CURE or SOLUTION...HOW FAR WILL MAN GO TO COMPLETE HIS DESTRUCTION...IS BEYOND A COMPUTER'S ROBOT DEDUCTION!"

HSR

THE MASTERPIECE

Framed by the vast unlimited sky
Bordered by mighty waters,
Sheltered by beautiful woodland groves,
Scented with flowers that bloom, and die
Protected by giant mountain peaks
The lands of "The Great Unknown"—
Snow-capped and towering—a nameless place
That beckons man on as the gold he seeks.
Bubbling with life and earthly joys
Reeking with pain and mortal strife
Dotted with wealth and material gains
Built on ideals of girls and boys
Streaked with blood, crime's banner unfurled
Stands out the masterpiece of art—
Painted by the one great God
A Picture of The World!
       HES

HEAVEN AND EARTH ARE MAN'S TO POSSESS

Rich are they who read and believe
For treasure untold is theirs to receive
Heaven and earth are man's to possess
For God made man just a little bit less
Than all His angels who already inherit
The untold riches that man too can merit
For it matters not what man's guilty of
He cannot go beyond God's love
And God in love forgives all sinners
And makes the poorest losers winners
God never refuses the earnest plea
Of those who constantly disagree
That there could be a living God
Who owns the sea, the sky, the sun
Who is ready and willing to share
the wealth and riches that abound everywhere
For the rich and poor and the young and old
Are all joint heirs of God's wealth untold.

THIS IS ALL MINE

It is true I'm not rich
    with silver or gold
And yet I'm convinced
    I have riches untold
For here I am standing
    on earth that is mine
That came as a gift
    with no mortgage to sign.
Mine to have, develop, and
    hold
Through a poem to write
    Or tale to be told.
God's country abounds in
    treasures galore
And thanks need be given
To Him, evermore.

GOD KEEP YOUR MIGHTY HAND ON AMERICA

God give us men with SPIRIT and DRIVE
To keep our ideals and faith alive
Not "driven men" whose purpose and goal
Is to feed their egos and not their soul
Who greedily reach and try to attain
Positions of POWER AND PROFIT AND GAIN...
But give us men with great spiritual drive
Who unselfishly work that all men may survive
And make this nation's deepest desire
To raise our standards and ethics higher
So all of the world and not just a few
Can live on earth as you want us to
Look with mercy on this "GREAT GOOD LAND"
And keep us a nation led by THY HAND!

THE PRAYER FOR PEACE

Our Father, up in heaven,
        hear this fervent prayer—
May the people of All Nations
        be United in Thy Care,
For earth's peace and man's salvation
        can come only by Thy grace
And not through bombs and missiles
        and our quest for outer space...
For until all men recognize
        that "The Battle Is The Lord's"
And peace on earth cannot be won
        with strategy and swords,
We will go on vainly fighting,
        as we have in ages past,
Finding only empty victories
        and a peace that cannot last...
But we've grown so rich and mighty
        and so arrogantly strong,
We no longer ask in humbleness—
        "God, show us where we're wrong"...
We have come to trust completely
        in the power of man-made things,
Unmindful of God's mighty power
        and that He is "King Of Kings"...
We have turned our eyes away from Him
        to go our selfish way,
And money, power and pleasure
        are the gods we serve today...
And the good green earth God gave us
        to peacefully enjoy,
Through greed and fear and hatred
        we are seeking to destroy...
Oh, Father, up in heaven,
        stir and wake our sleeping souls,
Renew our faith and lift us up
        and give us higher goals,
And grant us heavenly guidance
        as war threatens us again—
For, more than Guided Missiles,
        all the world needs Guided Men.

AN INDEPENDENCE DAY PRAYER

God bless America and keep us safe and free.
Safe from "all our enemies" wherever they may be—
For enemies are forces that often dwell within.
Things that seem so harmless become a major sin,
Little acts of selfishness grow into lust and greed
And make the love of power our idol and our creed...
For all our wealth and progress are as worthless as can be
Without the FAITH that made us great
       and kept our nation free,
And while it's hard to understand the complexities of war,
Each one of us must realize that we are fighting for
The principles of freedom and for the decency of man,
But all of this must be achieved according to God's Plan..
So help us as Americans to search deep down inside
And discover if the things we do are always justified,
And teach us to walk humbly and closer in Thy ways
And give us faith and courage
       and put purpose in our days,
And make each one of us aware that each must do his part
For in the individual is where peace must have its start...
For a BETTER WORLD to live in where all are safe and free
Must start with FAITH and HOPE
       and LOVE deep in the heart of "ME."

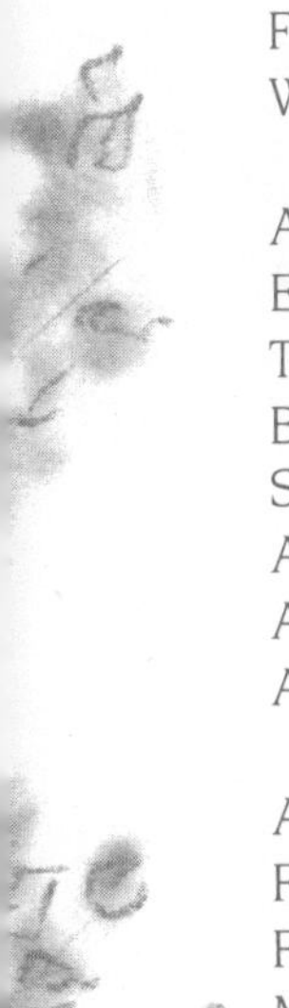

I COME TO MEET YOU

I come to MEET YOU, GOD, and as I linger here,
        I seem to feel YOU very near
A rustling leaf...a rolling slope...
        speaks to my heart of endless HOPE
The SUN JUST RISING IN THE SKY,
        the waking birdlings as they fly
The GRASS ALL WET WITH MORNING DEW,
        are telling me I'VE JUST MET YOU!
And gently thus the day is born
        and NIGHT gives way to BREAKING MORN
And once again I've MET YOU GOD,
        and worshipped on "YOUR HOLY SOD"
For WHO CAN SEE THE DAWN BREAK THROUGH
        WITHOUT A GLIMPSE OF HEAVEN AND YOU....
For WHO BUT GOD COULD MAKE THE DAY....
        and SOFTLY PUT THE NIGHT AWAY.

FAITH IS NOT A FOE TO SCIENCE

The higher into space man goes
The more he learns, the less he knows
For the wonderment of God abounds
And all His handiwork surrounds
The endless mystery of the skies
And all that silently beyond them lies
FOR FAITH IS NOT A FOE TO SCIENCE...
They're linked in very close alliance
And as men seek and search to find
The answer to the FINITE MIND
They also find that more and more
DISCOVERY is AN OPEN DOOR
To FAITH IN THE ALMIGHTY ONE...
Who made the sky and sea and sun.

110

GOD OF CREATION
SAVE OUR NATION

GREAT GOD THE FATHER
          OF ALL CREATION,
     LOOK DOWN UPON THIS
          STRIFE-TORN NATION,
     REVIVE OUR SPIRITS LAIN
          DORMANT SO LONG,
     RENEW OUR FAITH AND
          KEEP IT STRONG,
FORGIVE OUR ARROGANCE
          AND GREED
     AND GUIDE US IN THIS HOUR
          OF NEED—
HAND OF GOD REACH OUT
          ONCE MORE
     AND WITH THE "BREATH
          OF LIFE" RESTORE
YOUR SPIRIT IN THE FLESH
          OF MEN
     SO WE MAY LIVE
          IN PEACE AGAIN—
FOR MANKIND'S FUTURE
          AND SURVIVAL
     DEPEND ALONE ON THE
          SPIRIT'S REVIVAL!

GOD GAVE MAN THE EARTH TO ENJOY—NOT TO DESTROY

"The earth is the Lord's and the fullness thereof"—
He gave it to man as a Gift of His Love
So all men might live as He hoped that they would,
Sharing together all things that were good...
But man only destroyed "the good earth of God"—
He polluted the air and ravished the sod.
He cut down the forest with ruthless disdain.
And the earth's natural beauty he perverted for gain...
And all that God made and all that He meant
To bring man great blessings and a life of content
Have only made man a "giant of greed"
In a world where the password is "SEX, SIN and SPEED"...

And now in an age filled with violent dissent
Man finds he's imprisoned in his own discontent—
He has taken the earth that God placed in man's care
And built his own "hell" without being aware
That the future we face was fashioned by man
Who in ignorance resisted GOD'S BEAUTIFUL PLAN,
And what God created to be paradise
Became by man's lust and perversion and vice
A "caldron of chaos" in a "fog of pollution"
To which man can find no cure or solution—
How far man will go to complete his destruction
Is beyond a computer's robot deduction.

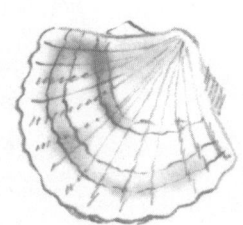

LITTLE BOY—TO MANHOOD

It only seems like yesterday
        that you were a "little boy"—
Cute and sweet and "huggable,"
        your parents' pride and joy...
But now you are a young man
        who has helplessly been hurled
Into a "seething struggle"
        of a violent, changing world...
So remember as a member
        of "OUR YOUNGER GENERATION"
It's your morals and ideals
        that will help rebuild "OUR NATION."

NOVEMBER 22, 1963—
THERE ARE NO WORDS

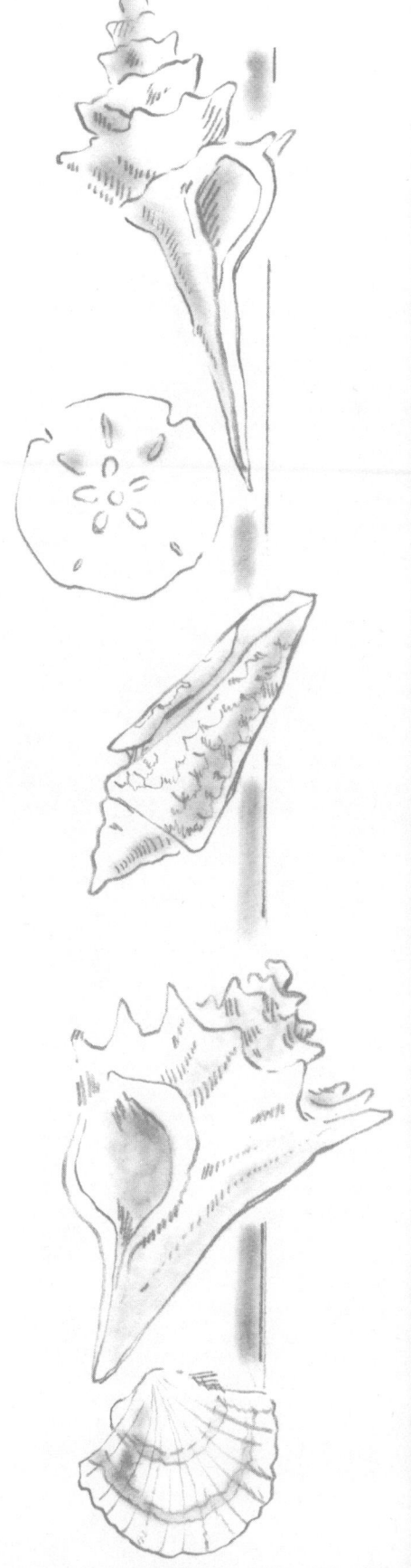

Our shock is too great,
    Our grief is too new,
Our emotions too mixed,
    Our small words too few
To capture and phrase
    in a fitting expression
All that we've learned
    from this grim, tragic lesson...
So, while grief is so keen
    and emotion so great,
Let us kneel down in prayer
    as our souls meditate
On the part that we played
    in our nation's decay
That brought us in sorrow
    to this world-shaking day...
Let us search our own souls
    and look deep inside
And see written there
    our vain, selfish pride,
For the struggle ahead
    is centered within,
Each man has his own
    private battle to win,
And above the drum's roll
    and the unrestrained tears
May the words of the Lord
    ring clear in our ears—
"Love one another"
    and help those in need,
Regardless of color
    of race, church or creed,
And keep us both humble
    and grateful, dear God,
Aware of those sleeping
    'neath Arlington's sod,
And strengthen the bonds
    that join us with others
So all men may live
    in peace with their brothers...
Forgive our transgressions
    and "Be with us yet"
"Lest we forget! Lest we forget!"

7

Helen, the Benefactor

Perhaps the least known
aspect of the life of Helen Steiner
Rice was her benefactions.

They were many and varied,
to people in all walks of life,
across color lines, and
ecumenical in outreach.

Her checks, usually noted in
the postscript of a letter, served
to put students through college,
buy clothing for the needy,
preserve churches, and spread
the Word. Even when her health
was failing, her spirit remained
indomitable. She wrote letters;
she called when she could not
call on friends; she prayed; she
persisted; and through it all she
loved.

"There are three things that
remain—faith, hope, and
love—and the greatest of
these is love. Let love be your
greatest aim...."

Love was her legacy.

Remembering Helen

Helen Steiner Rice's poetry was but one means by which she touched the lives of many people. She spent numerous hours corresponding with sick and despairing persons, giving them comfort and cheer. Additionally, monetary rewards which she received as a result of her artistic talents were generously shared with others. She made extraordinary contributions to churches—not only her own, but many that were located in poor neighborhoods where a special need was brought to her attention. She was particularly cognizant of the needs of the elderly and the poor and repeatedly aided their causes. In one instance, she paid weekly visits to encourage a blind friend. The creation of her Foundation was for the specific purpose of providing continued assistance to those who needed help. Helen Steiner Rice's life was a sequence of giving. Her love for her fellowman will long survive her years on earth.

Eugene P. Ruehlmann
Co-Trustee,
The Helen Steiner Rice Foundation

Dear Rev. B —

...This is one subject I am rabidly opinionated on. People always have money to buy an extra package of cigarettes or a couple more cocktails or see a sexy movie. But when it comes to GOD, they always feel HE will be satisfied with the "dregs."

I intend to make my little talk on the subject of "BEYOND OUR ASKING" and tell them that GOD can give more than anyone could ask for. Yet we find it so difficult to give HIM anything. HE gives "BEYOND ALL OUR ASKING!" Why can't we honor HIM by doing the same thing? GOD offers the "GREATEST GIFT" to mankind in the world, and only a seemingly few try, in any way, to repay HIM.

HSR

Dear Rev. B —

...My secretary tells me I am "paid up" for all the Sundays through March. But I will be sending you an EASTER CHECK later this month. Today, however, I am enclosing a check for [you] to use on one of [your] "PET PROJECTS."...

HSR

Dear Rev. B —

...I'm so glad you told me that G — needed a little assistance. I have never made a better investment, for faithfully that girl has written to me and told me how she's getting along at college. I am just honored and happy to have had a little part in making it possible for her to be studying for the ministry....

HSR

Dear Rev. B —

...You know, it really saddens me sometimes that I neglect dear friends and cannot find the time to write to the people who mean the most to me. But I do realize that TIME IS RUNNING OUT FOR ME. I have only one goal and one aim in life, and that is to do as much as I can to make this a better world in which to live before I leave for "WIDER FIELDS OF USEFULNESS."...

HSR

A SPRINGTIME PRAYER

God grant this little Springtime prayer
And make our hearts grown cold with care
Once more aware of the waking earth
Now pregnant with life and bursting with birth—
For how can man feel any fear or doubt
When on every side all around and about
The March winds blow across man's face
And whisper of God's power and grace—
Oh, give us faith to believe again
That peace on earth, good will to men
Will follow this "Winter of man's mind"
And awaken his heart and make him kind—
And just as Great Nature sends the Spring
To give new birth to each sleeping thing,
God grant rebirth to man's "slumbering soul"
And help him forsake his selfish goal.

SPIRITUAL BOND

I am planning to walk
        on a "path yet untrod,"
Content that my future
        will be determined by God.
But it doesn't take Christmas
        to make me remember,
Nor are my GOOD WISHES
        confined to DECEMBER.
But as day follows day
        and thought follows thought,
I'll think of the JOY
        that YOUR FRIENDSHIP has brought,
And may the books I have written
        and the words I have spoken
Be a "SPIRITUAL BOND"...
        UNCHANGED and UNBROKEN.

EXPECTATION! ANTICIPATION! REALIZATION!

God gives us a power we so seldom employ
For we're so unaware it is filled with such joy
For the gift that God gives us is ANTICIPATION
Which we can FULFILL with SINCERE EXPECTATION
For there's power in BELIEF when we think we will find
JOY for the heart and sweet peace for the mind
For believing the day will bring a surprise
Is not only pleasant but surprisingly wise...
For we open the door to let joy walk through
When we learn to expect the "BEST" and "MOST", too
For believing we'll find a happy surprise
Makes REALITY out of a FANCIED SURMISE!

HOW TO FIND HAPPINESS
THROUGH THE YEAR

Everybody, everywhere
        seeks happiness, it's true,
But finding it and keeping it
        seems difficult to do,
Difficult because we think
        that happiness is found
Only in the places where
        wealth and fame abound—
And so we go on searching
        in "palaces of pleasure"
Seeking recognition
        and monetary treasure,
Unaware that happiness
        is just a "state of mind"
Within the reach of everyone
        who takes time to be kind—
For in making OTHERS HAPPY
        we will be happy, too,
For the happiness you give away
        returns to "shine on you."

I'M OLD-FASHIONED

Although the world would have us think
  It's "stylish to be smart"

And act sophisticated
  And camouflage the heart,

I'm one of the old-fashioned few
  Who think that deep inside

Behind our "suave defenses"
  Of vanity and pride

There is a LONELY LONGING
  For LOVE that's UNEXPRESSED

Because we think it's fashionable
  To keep sentiment repressed!

WE SHOULD DO IT "HIS WAY"

As LONG AS THERE ARE HATE AND GREED AND LUST IN THE
HEART, PEACE CANNOT COME TO US EVEN THOUGH WE PRAY
FOR IT...FOR WE CANNOT HAVE A UNITED NATION WHEN
MAN'S HEART IS SINFUL.

THE FAITH OF OUR PILGRIM FATHERS WAS BORN OF
NEED AND DESPERATION. BUT TODAY WE ARE AFFLUENT
AND SELF-SATISFIED, AND WE ALL HAVE TOO MUCH OF
EVERYTHING.

SO, WE FEEL NO NEED TO THANK GOD AT ALL, FOR, AS
THE SONG GOES, "WE DID IT OUR WAY."

THERE'S ONLY ONE WAY TO GET BACK TO GOD, AND THAT
IS TO REALIZE THAT HE IS THE CREATOR OF ALL LIFE
AND THE GIVER OF ALL BLESSINGS.

YOUR REWARD

It isn't WISE to ECONOMIZE
        when SPENDING for THE LORD—
GIVE HIM HIS SHARE
        and a little to SPARE
AND GREAT will be your reward!

DAILY THOUGHTS FOR
DAILY NEEDS

If we put our problems in God's hand,
There is nothing we need understand—
It is enough to just believe
That what we need we will receive.

Life is a mixture of sunshine and rain,
Teardrops and laughter, pleasure and pain—
We can't have all bright days, but it's certainly true
There was never a cloud that
The Sun Didn't Shine Through!

The more you love, the more you'll find
That life is good and friends are kind...
For only What We Give Away
Enriches Us from Day to Day.

Often we stand at life's crossroads
And view what we think is the end,
But God has a much bigger vision
And HE tells us it's "ONLY A BEND."

Everything is by comparison,
Both the BITTER and the SWEET,
And it takes a bit of both of them
To make our life complete.

Oh, make us more aware, dear God,
Of little daily graces
That come to us with "sweet surprise"
From never-dreamed-of places!

You can't pluck a rose all fragrant with dew
Without part of the fragrance
        remaining on you!

God never sends the WINTER
        without the JOY of SPRING...
And though today your heart may "cry"—
        tomorrow it will "SING!"

HE LOVES YOU!

It's amazing and incredible,
But it's as true as it can be,
God loves and understands us all
And that means YOU and ME—
His grace is all sufficient
For both the YOUNG and OLD,
For the lonely and the timid,
For the brash and for the bold—
His love knows no exceptions,
So never feel excluded,
No matter WHO or WHAT you are
Your name has been included—
And no matter what your past has been,
Trust God to understand,
And no matter what your problem is
Just place it in His Hand—
For in all of our UNLOVELINESS
This GREAT GOD LOVES US STILL.
He loved us since the world began
And what's more, HE ALWAYS WILL!